Praise for Marc Levy
and
Just Like Heaven

"While transcendental love between a living individual and
the soul of another (en route to a better place) has been
attempted in fiction and film, rarely has this plot device
worked. Marc Levy, in his debut novel, however, has
masterfully presented this impossible scenario."
—*New York Post*

"Entertaining and inspiring."
—*Rendezvous*

"A beautiful love story that will appeal to fans of romance,
supernatural fiction, and adult fairy tales."
—barnesandnoble.com

"Sparkles with terrific humor. . . . A memorable romance
that has a stunning cast of characters."
—*The Belles & Beaux of Romance*

"This novel is a whimsical, beautiful adult fairy tale that
will touch the hearts of its audience . . . an inspiring love
story that is an uplifting testament to the human spirit."
—*Affaire de Coeur*

"At first glance, the premise looks
preposterous. . . . But don't underestimate a
novice's intuitive skill. . . . Do whatever it takes to
give yourself permission to suspend disbelief."
—*St. Petersburg Times* (FL)

Just Like Heaven

Previously published as *If Only It Were True*

A NOVEL

Marc Levy

ATRIA BOOKS

New York London Toronto Sydney

ATRIA BOOKS

1230 Avenue of the Americas
New York, NY 10020

Library of Congress Catalog Card Number: 00703228

ISBN-13: 978-0-7434-0617-8
ISBN-10:   0-7434-0617-6
ISBN-13: 978-0-7432-9632-8 (Pbk)
ISBN-10:   0-7432-9632-X (Pbk)

This Atria Books trade paperback edition December 2005

1   3   5   7   9   10   8   6   4   2

For Louis

Part
ONE

June

Chapter
ONE

*T*he alarm clock sitting on the pale wood nightstand sounded at five-thirty. Curled under a down comforter in the middle of her large iron bed, Lauren opened her eyes to the clear golden dawn light that is so rare in San Francisco.

Lauren's apartment had an unusually pleasant air to it. Set on the top floor of a Victorian house on Green Street, it had an open-plan kitchen and living room, a big bedroom, a walk-in closet, and a vast bathroom with a large window. The floor was laid with wide slats of parquet; in the bathroom, this had been bleached and stenciled with a black checkerboard design. The white walls were hung with old drawings that Lauren had picked up in the galleries on Union Street. The ceiling was edged in wooden moldings finely carved by a skilled carpenter in the late 1900s; Lauren had stained them the color of light tea.

Coconut-fiber rugs edged in jute lay in the dining area

and by the fireplace. A big, inviting sofa upholstered in off-white cotton faced the hearth. The few pieces of furniture were dominated by unusually attractive lamps with pleated shades, which Lauren had acquired, one by one, over the past three years.

Lauren loved her apartment. It was the first home that had ever been truly hers—purchased with the inheritance her father, who had died when she was very young, had left her. She knew that her father would have loved this place, loved to watch the sailboats in the bay, whereas sometimes she felt her mother only loved the idea that her daughter might at last be settling down. Hah! She wished. Lauren's schedule in the past two years hadn't much improved since the slave hours of her internship. Still, she had devoted her few moments of leisure to decorating her apartment, to make it feel like her own.

So, once again, it had been a very short night. Lauren was a resident at San Francisco Memorial Hospital, and yesterday's tour of duty had lasted well beyond the usual twenty-four hours because of a last-minute influx of burn victims from a major fire. The first ambulances had roared into the emergency entrance ten minutes before she was due to stop work. Lauren had begun dispatching the wounded to surgery, under the panicked eyes of her team, without waiting for the relief doctor to arrive. With the swift, practiced moves of an experienced emergency-room doctor, she'd checked the vital signs of each patient, stuck a colored label on each chart indicating the severity of the victim's condition, assigned a preliminary diagnosis, ordered up the first tests, and directed the orderlies to the appropriate areas. The sixteen victims had arrived between midnight and 12:15. Screening was complete at 12:30, and by 12:45, teams of surgeons who had been recalled for the emergency had begun the first operations of this grueling night.

Lauren had assisted her supervisor, Dr. Fernstein, through two successive operations. She had not left until well after two, when Fernstein had ordered her home, warning her that if fatigue got the better of her she could endanger her patients' lives.

She had driven through the deserted city streets at the wheel of her antique Triumph convertible. "I'm too tired and I'm driving too fast," she'd repeated to herself, over and over, fighting the urge to sleep. The idea of returning to the emergency room on a stretcher was enough to keep her alert.

Lauren had activated the remote control to the garage door and parked the old car. Taking the interior stairs, she had bounded up them four at a time, relieved to be home.

Blearily entering the kitchen, Lauren had started absent-mindedly shedding her clothes as she made herself some herbal tea. The jars that embellished the shelf held every type and flavor, as though there were a special herbal aroma for every moment of the day. She had set her cup on the nightstand, climbed into bed, and instantly fallen asleep. Once again, her day had been much too long.

She was certainly exhausted enough to deserve a morning in bed, but she would nonetheless need to make an early start. Taking advantage of a two-day break that for once coincided with the weekend, Lauren had accepted an invitation to stay with friends in Carmel, and nothing could make her renounce the beauty of an early-morning drive down Route 1. Lauren loved that stretch of the Pacific Coast Highway between San Francisco and Monterey, loved seeing the sun crest the high coastal hills and sparkle on the cold Pacific below.

Lauren's dog, Kali, leaped onto the bed as she felt her mistress stir. "Don't look at me like that—I don't even feel human yet!" she told the dog. "And, honey, I'm abandoning you for two days. Mom will come by to get you around eleven. Move over. I'll get up and make breakfast."

Lauren uncurled her legs, stretched out her arms, yawned widely, pulled on a T-shirt, and jumped to her feet. Rubbing at her hair, she moved behind the kitchen counter, opened the fridge, yawned again, and took out butter, jam, crispbread, a can of dog food, an open packet of Parma ham, a chunk of Gouda, coffee, two cartons of milk, a bowl of applesauce, two plain yogurts, cereal, half a grapefruit; the other half remained on the bottom shelf. Kali watched her, nodding her head urgently. Lauren glared back and exclaimed, "I know—but I'm hungry!"

As usual, she made Kali's breakfast first, in a heavy earthenware bowl. Then she assembled her own tray and headed for her desk.

From the window, if she tilted her head a little, she could see the Golden Gate Bridge, suspended like a hyphen between the two sides of the bay, and beyond it the houses that clung to the hills of Sausalito, and the marina of Tiburon. Directly below her, roofs descended like steps toward the Marina. She opened the window wide: the city was still sleeping. Only the booming foghorns of the big freighters shipping out to China, mixed with the cries of seagulls, disturbed this languid morning. She stretched again, then tucked into her breakfast with a hearty appetite. She had had no time for dinner last night. Three times she'd tried to take a bite of her sandwich, but each time her beeper had shrilly summoned her to a new emergency.

When people asked Lauren what it was like to work in the ER, she invariably quipped, "Relaxing."

After devouring most of her feast, she put the tray in the sink and headed for the bathroom. She slid her fingers down the Venetian blinds to push the wooden slats shut, let her cotton T-shirt fall to the floor, and stepped under the powerful warm jet of the shower. Now she was properly awake.

Lauren wrapped a towel around her waist, looked in the mirror, made a face, and decided in favor of a little makeup. She threw on a pair of jeans and a polo shirt, took off the jeans and put on a skirt, took off the skirt and pulled the jeans back on. She took a canvas bag from the closet and stuffed in a few toiletries and some clothes. She was ready for the weekend. She eyed the hopeless disorder around her—clothes on the floor, towels scattered, dirty dishes in the sink, the bed unmade—and glared at her household objects decisively. She said aloud, "Not a word! No complaining! I'll be back tomorrow evening and I'll straighten you all up for the week."

Then she took a pencil and paper and wrote a note, which she stuck to the refrigerator door with a large frog-shaped magnet:

Mom
   Thanks for looking after the dog, please don't clean up, I'll take care of it when I get back.
   I'll pick up Kali from your place Sunday around five.
   Love you. Your favorite physician.

She slipped on her coat and patted her dog tenderly. "Sorry, Kali. I need a break. Be good!" She planted a kiss on Kali's forehead and slammed the door shut.

She walked down to the main door, took the outside stairs to the garage, and jumped into her aging convertible.

"I'm off, I'm really off!" she said to herself and her car. "I can hardly believe it—what a miracle. Now you have to agree to start. And I'm warning you, if you cough just one time I'll drown your motor in maple syrup and turn you over to the junkyard. I'll replace you with a young car loaded with electronics, with no choke and no tantrums on cold mornings. Got that straight? Go!"

The ring of conviction in her voice must have impressed the old English car, for its engine came alive on the first twist of the key. It was going to be a beautiful day.

Chapter
TWO

*L*auren eased the Triumph onto the street quietly. She didn't want to wake her neighbors on Green Street, on this pretty block lined with trees and old houses, where people knew one another by sight, as in a village. Six crossroads before Van Ness—one of the two main arteries through the city—she tuned her radio to 101.3 FM and sped up. The pale morning light shifted color every few minutes, progressively illuminating a series of spectacular views of the city. Lauren loved the thrilling vertigo of racing across San Francisco's steep hills.

As she made a tight left onto Post Street she heard an odd noise—a rattling—stemming perhaps from the transmission. Probably nothing, she thought as she zoomed down the steep slope toward Union Square. It was six-thirty in the morning, Bruce Springsteen was blaring—Lauren was happy, happier than she had been for a very long time. Good-bye to stress;

good-bye to the hospital. She sang along with Bruce. This would be a weekend of her very own, and there wasn't a minute to lose.

Union Square was quiet. In a few hours the sidewalks would be spilling over with tourists and locals, shopping in the department stores around the square. Cable cars would file up and down, shop windows would light up, and a long line of cars would form at the entrance to the parking garage under the public gardens, where bands of street musicians would be playing for quarters and the occasional dollar.

But for now, on this early weekend morning, calm reigned. The storefronts were dark. A few homeless people slept still on their benches, and the parking-lot attendant dozed in his booth at the entrance to the underground garage. The Triumph was sailing as Lauren shifted gears. The lights were green all the way. She felt exhilarated as the morning air buffeted her head scarf. She shifted down to second gear as she approached her turn onto Geary in front of the vast facade of the Macy's building. A perfect turn, the tires squealing softly, and then a strange noise, a series of clicks, everything moving fast now. The clicking became a blur of conflicting metallic sounds.

A sudden bang! Time stopped. All dialogue ceased between the steering and the wheels. The car swerved and skidded on the damp surface. Lauren's face tensed; her hands gripped the useless steering wheel. It offered no resistance, spinning in a limbo of its own. The Triumph continued gliding. Time seemed to ease into its own rhythm, stretching out now into an infinitely long yawn. Lauren felt her head spin—no, it was the scene around her that was spinning—at astonishing speed. Then the Triumph's wheels slammed into the curb. The front of the car rose into the embrace of a fire hydrant. The hood arched up further still. In one last effort, the car rotated on its axis and ejected its driver, by now much too heavy for its gravity-defying backflip. Lauren's body was hurled into the air, then crashed back down against Macy's huge display window, which exploded into thousands of glass shards.

Lauren rolled on the sidewalk, then came to rest on the blanket of glass and debris, while the old Triumph ended its performance, and its long career, on its back, half on the sidewalk. A plume of steam rose from its entrails, and it breathed its ladylike last.

Lauren lay still. She was peaceful, almost serene. Her features were smooth, her breathing slow and even. There might have been a small smile on her slightly parted lips. Her eyes were closed—she seemed to be sleeping. Her long hair framed her face; her right hand lay across her midriff.

In his booth, the parking-lot attendant blinked hard. He'd witnessed it all, "just like in the movies," only this time "it was for real," he'd later say. He rose, ran outside, then changed his mind, turned around, frantically pulled at the phone and dialed 911.

Help was on its way.

*T*he dining hall of San Francisco Memorial Hospital was a large room, with white-tiled floor and walls painted yellow. Several rectangular Formica tables lay along a central path leading to machines dispensing soda, coffee, and sandwiches, and Dr. Philip Stern sprawled over one of the tables, a cold cup of coffee near his hand. A little farther away a colleague was rocking on a chair, eyes lost in thought. The beeper rang deep in Stern's pocket. He opened one eye and looked at his watch with a groan; his shift would end in fifteen minutes. "Damn, I have the worst luck—Frank, call reception."

Frank caught the wall phone beside him, listened for a moment, then turned back to Stern. "Up you get, pal. It's ours, Union Square, code three, seems serious." The two ER residents got up and headed for the entryway, where the ambulance was waiting for them, its lights dazzling and engine running. Two short blasts of the siren marked the departure of Unit 2. It was 6:45 AM; Stockton Street was completely deserted, and the ambulance raced through the early morning.

"Shit, and it looks like it'll be a nice day."

"What's with the whining?"

"I'm beat, and I need sleep, and I'm not going to get it."

"Turn left, there's no one on the road, we'll go up the one-way street."

Frank turned, and the ambulance headed up Post Street toward Union Square. "Hey, speed up, I can see it." When they got to the square, the two doctors spotted the carcass of the old Triumph splayed across the hydrant. Frank cut the siren.

"Wow, he really totaled that," Stern said, whistling, jumping out of the ambulance.

Two policemen were already on the scene, and one of them directed Stern toward the broken window.

"Where is he?" the resident asked.

"There, in front of you, it's a woman, and she's a doctor, in the emergency room apparently. You recognize her?"

Already kneeling beside Lauren's body, Stern yelled at his colleague to come quickly. Using scissors, he cut through jeans and T-shirt to the naked skin. Her long left leg was twisted and bruised, indicating a fracture. The rest of the body had no apparent wounds.

"Let's get an EKG and start an IV. I've got a thready pulse and no blood pressure, respiration forty-eight, head wound, looks like a closed fracture of the left femur with internal hemorrhage. Get me two units. Do we know her? Is she one of us?"

"I've seen her. She's a resident in ER—works with Fern-stein. A tough cookie. Stands up to his bullying."

Philip didn't react to this last remark. Frank pasted the seven electrodes onto the young woman's chest, connecting each one with a different-colored wire to the portable electro-cardiograph. He switched it on, and the screen instantly leaped to life.

"What's it show?" he asked Philip.

"Nothing good; she's going. Pressure, eighty over sixty; pulse, a hundred and forty; lips are blue. I'll start preparing a number-seven endotracheal tube. We'll need to intubate."

Dr. Stern finished hooking the IV catheter into Lauren's arm and handed the bag of saline solution to one of the policemen.

"Hold that good and high, I need both hands."

Turning briefly to his partner, he directed him to inject 5 milligrams of epinephrine and 125 milligrams of Solumedrol into the IV, and to prepare the defibrillator. Lauren's temperature now began to fall rapidly. The tracing on the EKG was becoming erratic. A small red heart began to blink at the bottom of the green screen, accompanied instantly by a short, urgent beep—a warning that heart failure was imminent.

"Hang in there, sweetie! She must be pissing blood inside. How's the belly?"

"Soft. She's probably bleeding in the leg. Ready to intubate?"

They secured an airway in under a minute. Stern asked for a report on vital signs; Frank replied that respiration was still stable, but pressure had fallen to fifty. He had no time to finish his sentence: the short beep was replaced by a shrill alarm from the machine.

"That's it, she's in V-Fib. Give me three hundred joules."

Philip picked up the two paddles of the apparatus and rubbed them together.

"Go ahead, you have the juice," yelled Frank.

"Pull back, I'm hitting her."

Jolted by the electric shock, the body arched brutally before falling back.

"Nope, no good."

"Try three-sixty, let's go!"

"Three-sixty it is, go ahead!"

"Pull back!"

The body again rose and fell back lifelessly. "Give me another five of epinephrine and reload to three-sixty. Pull back!" Another jolt; another spasmodic leap. "Still fibrillating! We're losing her: inject one unit of lidocaine into the IV and reload. Pull back!" The body heaved upward. "Give her an amp of bicarb and reload to three-eighty stat!"

Lauren received yet another shock. Her heart seemed to respond to the drugs. It returned to normal rhythm; but not for long. The alarm signal, which had briefly ceased, shrilled out louder than ever. "Cardiac arrest!" Frank yelled.

Immediately, Philip began cardiac massage. He was unusually determined to save this patient. As he worked to bring her back to life, he begged her, "Don't be an idiot. It's a fine day. Come back. Don't do this to us!"

He ordered his partner to reload the machine once more. Frank tried to calm him down. "Let her go, Philip, it's no good." But Stern would not give up; he yelled at Frank to reload the defibrillator. His partner yielded. Yet again Philip shouted, "Pull back!" and once more the body arched. But the electrocardiogram remained stubbornly flat.

Philip went back to cardiac massage, his forehead beaded with sweat. A sense of despair at his powerlessness was made worse by his sheer exhaustion. As Frank looked on, it occurred to him that Philip was losing his grip on reality. He should have stopped everything minutes ago and pronounced the time of death. But nothing, it seemed, could stop him: he went on massaging Lauren's heart.

"Give another shot of epinephrine and go up to four hundred joules."

"Philip, stop it, it makes no sense. She's dead. This is a waste of time."

"Shut up and do what I tell you!"

The policeman looked questioningly at the doctor kneeling beside Lauren, but Philip was focusing on his patient. Frank shrugged, injected another dose into the IV tubing, and reloaded the defibrillator. He called out the threshold level of four hundred joules, and Stern delivered it, without even giving the warning to pull back. Jolted by the current, the torso jerked violently upward. The EKG remained hopelessly flat-line. The resident did not look at it. He pounded his fist on Lauren's chest. "Damn! Damn!"

Frank grabbed him by the shoulders and shook him. "Philip, you're losing it, buddy. You're cracking up here. You need a rest. Calm down. Give me the time of death and we'll pack up."

Philip was sweating, his eyes haggard. Frank raised his voice, gripped his friend's face in his hands, forced him to stare him in the eyes. He ordered him to calm down; when Philip didn't react, he slapped him. When the young doctor finally focused, Frank said calmly, "Come back to me, buddy. Get a grip." Then, at the end of his rope, he let go of his partner and got up, his eyes as vacant as Philip's. Spellbound, the policemen gazed at the two doctors. Frank was walking in circles, apparently at a complete loss. Philip, crumpled over on his knees, slowly raised his head and said in a low voice, "Time of death: seven-ten." He turned to the policeman who was still awkwardly holding the IV bag and said, "You can take her now. It's over. There's nothing more we can do for her."

Frank laid his arm across his partner's shoulder and walked him toward the ambulance.

The policemen gawked as the medics climbed in. "Those guys—they're not all there," noted one of them.

The second policeman stared at him. "You ever been on a job where one of us got killed?"

"No."

"Then you can't understand what those two have just been through. Come on, give me a hand, we'll get hold of her gently and put her on the stretcher in the van."

The ambulance had already disappeared around the corner. The two policemen lifted Lauren's inert body, set it on a stretcher, and covered it with a blanket. The few passersby who had stopped to view the scene wandered off.

Inside the ambulance, the two partners still hadn't said a word.

Frank broke the silence. "What got into you, Philip?"

"She's not even thirty years old—she's a doctor—she's drop-dead beautiful."

"And that's just what she did, she dropped dead. So what if she's a pretty doctor—she could have been ugly and worked in a Seven-Eleven. It's fate, and you can't do a thing about it. It was her time. When we get back, you grab some sleep and put all this shit behind you."

Two blocks behind them, the police van was headed for an intersection when a limo raced through a red light. Furious, the policeman braked sharply and sounded his siren. The limo driver stopped and babbled an apology. Lauren's body had been thrown off the stretcher by the sudden halt, so the two men went around to the rear of the van. The younger cop grabbed hold of Lauren's ankles while the older man took her arms. His expression froze when he looked at the young woman's chest.

"She's fuckin' breathing!"

"What?"

"She's breathing, I tell you. Get behind the wheel. Move it. We've got to get to the hospital."

"Jesus! I told you those two medics didn't look right."

"Shut up and drive. I don't know what's going on, but they're going to hear about it from me."

*T*he police van overtook the ambulance under the startled eyes of the two medics. Weren't those "their" cops? Philip wanted to turn the siren back on and follow them, but Frank refused—he was finished.

"Why are they driving like that?"

"Who knows?" said Frank. "Maybe it wasn't them. They all look alike."

Ten minutes later they pulled up at the entrance to the emergency unit and parked alongside the police van, whose doors were still open.

Philip went into the hospital and hurried toward the ER check-in desk. Skipping any preliminary greeting, he blurted out, "Did they just bring someone in?" Not waiting for a reply, he insisted, "Where is she?"

"The woman in the car accident?" asked the receptionist. "Area three. Fernstein's with her. Apparently she's one of his team."

Behind him, the older policeman tapped him on the shoulder. "What shit were you medics playing at?"

"I beg your pardon?"

How could he have pronounced a young woman dead when she was still breathing in his van? "You realize that if I hadn't noticed, we'd have put her into cold storage alive? You haven't heard the last of this."

Just then, Dr. Fernstein emerged from surgery. Seeming not to notice the officer, he spoke directly to the young doctor. "Stern, how many doses of epinephrine did you give that woman?"

"Five milligrams, four times."

The professor reprimanded Philip. There had been absolutely no call for such intensive resuscitation techniques. His conduct had been wantonly overzealous. Then Fernstein turned to the police officer and told him that Lauren had died well before Dr. Stern had announced the time of death. He added that the emergency team's only error had been an overeager attempt to revive the heart, at taxpayers' expense. To put an end to further discussion, Fernstein explained that the injected drugs had pooled around the pericardium. "When you slammed on the brakes, the medication flowed into her heart, which reacted to the chemicals and started to beat again." Unfortunately, that did not alter the fact that the victim was brain-dead. As soon as the cardiac drugs wore off, the heart would stop again—"if it hasn't already."

Fernstein suggested that the officer apologize to Dr. Stern for his inappropriate comments, then asked Stern to come and see him. The older cop turned to Philip and growled, "So it's not just cops who close ranks to protect their own. Don't bother to show me out." He turned on his heel and left the hospital building. Even though the double doors of the emergency bay had closed, you could hear the slam as he shut the van doors.

Stern remained standing, with his arms resting on the reception desk, squinting at the duty nurse. "What the hell's all this about?" She shrugged and reminded him that Dr. Fernstein was waiting.

Philip knocked at the half-open door. Fernstein told him to come in. Standing behind his desk, his back turned to Stern as he gazed out the window, he was obviously waiting for Stern to speak first. Philip admitted that he was puzzled by what the professor had told the policeman.

Fernstein interrupted him coldly. "Listen, Stern. I gave him an explanation to set his mind at ease, and to keep him from filing a report that might ruin your career. The way you handled that resuscitation was unacceptable for someone of your experience. You should know how to deal with death when it has to happen. We're not gods, and we're not responsible for destiny. That young woman was dead when you arrived on the scene, and you were trying too hard, for too long."

"But how do you explain that she started breathing again?"

"I can't explain it and I don't have to. We don't understand everything. She's dead, Dr. Stern. I can see you don't like it, but she's gone. I don't give a damn if her lungs are moving and her heart is beating on its own—her electroencephalograph is flat. This woman is irreversibly brain dead. We'll let things take their course and then send her down to the morgue. Period."

"But you can't do that—not with so much evidence! We have to try!"

Fernstein shook his head and raised his voice. Was Stern telling him what to do? Did Stern know how much it cost to keep a person in intensive care, even just for a day? Did he think the hospital would block one of its beds just to keep a vegetable artificially alive? He told Stern to grow up. He, Fernstein, would not force this woman's family to spend weeks at the side of an inert and brainless life-form that was being kept going only by machines. He would not be responsible for making such a decision, purely to satisfy one doctor's oversize ego.

Fernstein ordered Stern to get out of his sight and take a shower. The young doctor stood his ground and restated his argument with renewed vigor. When he had declared Lauren dead, the patient had been in cardiorespiratory arrest for several minutes. Her heart and lungs had stopped functioning. Yes, he *had* kept trying to bring her back, because for the first time in his medical career he had felt that this woman did not want to die. He told Fernstein that behind Lauren's open eyes he had sensed her struggling, refusing to go under.

And so he had fought alongside her—fought beyond reason—and, ten minutes later, against all logic and everything he had been taught, her heart had started beating. Her lungs had begun to inhale and exhale again. There had been a breath of life. "You're right, we're doctors, and we don't know everything. And she's a doctor, too."

He begged Fernstein to give Lauren a chance. There had been cases in which coma victims had come back to life inexplicably, after six months or more. The way she had recommenced breathing was already miraculous. Who cared how much it would cost? "Don't let her go," he pleaded. "She doesn't want to go—that's what she's telling us."

After a moment's silence, Fernstein replied, "Doctor Stern, Lauren was one of my students. She was a tough lady and a fine doctor. I had a lot of respect for her, and I thought she would go far. I also think you will go far. This conversation is now over."

Stern left the office without closing the door. Frank was waiting for him in the corridor.

"What are you doing here?"

"What the hell is wrong with you, Philip? Do you know who you were yelling at?"

"Yes. And?"

"He was that woman's professor. He's known her for fifteen months. He's saved more lives than you may in your entire career. You've got to get a grip on yourself, you're out of control."

"Give me a break, Frank. I've had enough lectures for one day."

Chapter
THREE

*D*r. Fernstein closed the door of his office, picked up the phone, hesitated, put it down, took a couple of steps toward the window, then grabbed the phone again. He asked for the surgical suite and was immediately connected.

"Fernstein speaking. Get everything ready. We're operating in ten minutes. I'll send up the chart."

He replaced the phone carefully, shook his head, and left his office. He found himself face to face with Professor Williams.

"How are you?" Williams asked. "Coffee?"

"Can't."

"What are you up to?"

"A fool's errand. I'm going to do something stupid. Got to go—I'll give you a call."

Fernstein entered the operating room wearing a close-fitting green scrub suit. A nurse pulled sterile gloves over his hands. The room was vast; the surgical team already surrounded Lauren's body. Behind her head, a monitor displayed the rhythm of her breathing and heartbeat.

"How are her vital signs?" Fernstein asked the anesthetist.

"Stable, unbelievably stable. Sixty-five and one-twenty over eighty. Her blood gases are normal. She's asleep—you can begin."

"She is, indeed, *asleep,* as you put it."

Fernstein's scalpel cut into Lauren's thigh for the length of the fracture. As he began to spread apart the muscle tissue, Fernstein addressed his team. Calling them "dear colleagues," he explained that they were about to see a professor of surgery with twenty years' experience perform an operation worthy of the skills of a second-year resident—setting a fractured femur.

"And do you know why I'm doing it? Because no self-respecting resident would perform such an operation on a patient who has been brain dead for more than two hours." He added that he would therefore appreciate it if nobody asked him any questions. Setting the broken leg would take fifteen minutes at most. He thanked them for going along with him on this one.

Lauren had been one of his students. All the medical staff present in the room knew her, knew how hard this must be for Fernstein. They were determined to help him through it.

A radiologist came in and mounted a CT scan on the view box. The images showed a blood clot on the brain. To relieve the pressure, a hole was drilled in the back of Lauren's skull and a fine needle passed through the meninges, monitored on a screen by the neurosurgeon, who directed it to the site of the hematoma. The brain itself appeared unharmed. Fluid began to drain through the tubing. Almost instantly, the intracranial pressure dropped. The anesthetist adjusted the respirator to increase the flow of oxygen to the brain. Once decompressed, the brain cells reverted to a normal metabolism, gradually eliminating the accumulated toxins. Minute by minute, the nature of the endeavor was changing. The whole team gradually forgot that they were operating on a person who was clinically dead. Everyone entered into the spirit of the task at hand, one skilled move following another. X-rays were taken, rib fractures repaired, and the area around the lung drained. The surgery was methodical and meticulous. Five hours later, Dr. Fernstein snapped his gloves off. He asked the team to close the incisions and transfer his patient to the recovery room. He ordered the nurses to take Lauren off the respirator once the anesthesia had worn off.

Once again he thanked the team for their help and their future discretion. Before leaving surgery, he asked one of the nurses, Betty, to let him know when she disconnected Lauren. Leaving the suite, he walked quickly toward the elevators. As he passed reception, he asked the duty nurse whether Dr. Stern was still in the building. The young woman replied that he wasn't: Dr. Stern had left, looking very low. He thanked her and walked on, telling her that he would be in his office if anyone needed him.

Lauren was taken from the operating room to recovery. Betty connected the cardiac monitor, the electroencephalograph, and the respirator. Thus arrayed, the young woman lying on the bed looked like an astronaut. The nurse took a blood sample and left the room. The sleeping patient looked peaceful; her eyelids seemed to trace the contours of a soft, deep universe of sleep. Half an hour went by, and Betty called Dr. Fernstein to say that Lauren's anesthesia had worn off. Her vital signs were stable. Betty wanted to be sure about the next step: she asked Dr. Fernstein to confirm his previous order.

"Disconnect the respirator. I'll be down in a while."

He hung up. Betty went back into the recovery room. She detached Lauren's breathing apparatus from the extension tubing that led to the machine, allowing her patient to try to breathe on her own. A few moments later she pulled out the tube altogether, freeing Lauren's throat. She brushed a strand of Lauren's hair back from her forehead, smiled tenderly at her, and went out, turning the light off behind her. The room was bathed in the faint green glow from the encephalograph machine. The line was still flat. It was precisely 9:30 PM, and everything was quiet.

At the end of the first hour, the EEG tracing began to wobble—very slightly at first. Suddenly, the needle jerked upward to delineate a sharp peak, then fell sharply downward before returning to the horizontal.

As fate would have it, no one witnessed this anomaly. An hour later Betty returned to the room. After checking Lauren's vital signs, she unrolled a few inches of the telltale strip of paper that the machine had generated. Betty noticed the strange peak, frowned, and read a few inches more. Since the rest of the tracing was flat-line, she threw the strip in the trash without further ado. She took the phone off the wall and called Fernstein.

"It's me. We're looking at a deep coma with vital signs stable. What do I do?"

"Find a bed on the fifth floor, and thanks, Betty."

Fernstein hung up.

Part
TWO

November

Chapter
FOUR

Arthur opened the door to the street-level garage with the remote control and parked his Saab. He climbed the interior staircase that led from the garage to his new third-floor apartment, swung the door shut with his foot, put his briefcase down, took off his coat, and collapsed onto the couch. There were more than a dozen cardboard boxes stacked in the living room, waiting to be unpacked. He had moved in only ten days ago, and he hadn't brought much with him—only his drafting table, a desk, his work files, his CDs, and his art and architecture books. Only after his relationship with Carol Ann had finally, definitively fallen apart had he accepted that it was time for him to move on, to try to start living his own life again, rather than the somewhat tentative, temporary one he'd grafted on to hers.

He'd been lucky to find this apartment. An architect specializing in the restoration of homes, he was amazed by how comfortable he'd immediately felt when he'd entered the place. Whoever had designed this environment had a keen sense of life and had created a home of taste and charm—and, coming from Arthur, this was a supreme compliment. He hadn't had to change anything—just fit his drafting table between the fireplace and the writing desk, buy some towels and linens and rudimentary kitchen supplies, and he'd had an instant home.

He changed his suit for a pair of jeans and started unpacking books and CDs, arranging them alphabetically on the shelf by the fireplace. When he finished, he folded up the boxes, vacuumed the floor, and sorted out the kitchen area. Finally, he looked around at his new nest. "I may be turning into a neat freak," he said to himself. Walking into the bathroom, he hesitated between a shower and a bath, opted for the bath, started the water running, switched on the little radio sitting on the radiator close by the walk-in closet, undressed, and sank into the tub with a sigh of relief.

As Peggy Lee sang "Fever" on 101.3 FM, Arthur dunked his head several times under the water. There was something odd about the acoustic quality of the song. The stereo effect was amazingly realistic—particularly since his radio had only one crummy internal speaker. He sat up straight in the bath and listened carefully. It sounded as though the finger-snapping that accompanied the tune came from the walk-in closet by the bathroom wall. Intrigued, he emerged from the water and crept over to the closet doors to investigate. The sound was more and more distinct. He paused, took a deep breath, and abruptly threw the doors open. His eyes widened, and he stumbled back.

Huddled on the floor beneath the hangers sat a young

woman, eyes closed, seemingly transported by the rhythm of the song, humming along to it and snapping her fingers.

"What are you doing here?" he asked, thrown completely off-guard. "Who are you?"

The woman jumped and looked at him, startled. "You can see me?"

"Of course I can see you."

She seemed bewildered. "You can hear me?"

He pointed out that he wasn't blind or deaf and asked again, "What are you doing here?"

"This is wonderful, it's just amazing!"

Arthur saw nothing "wonderful" about the situation, although there was plenty that was "amazing." Increasingly irritated, he asked her, for the third time, what she was doing in his bathroom in the middle of the night.

"I don't think you realize how amazing this is," she answered. "Touch my arm."

He stood there nonplussed as she held out her arm.

"Please . . ."

"No, I won't touch your arm. What's going on here?"

She took Arthur's wrist and asked him if he felt it when she touched him. Greatly exasperated, he confirmed that he did indeed feel her touch, that he saw her, and that he heard her perfectly well. For the fourth time, he asked her who she was and what she was doing in his bathroom closet. She ignored his question, and repeated, playfully, that it was "fabulous" that he could see her, hear her, touch her.

Arthur was exhausted after a long day. He was in no mood for games. "That's enough, lady. What is this, a practical joke? Who are you? A call girl from my partner, as a housewarming gift?"

"Are you always this rude? Do I look like a hooker?"

Arthur sighed. "No, you don't look like a hooker. You just happen to be hiding in my closet in the middle of the night."

"Right now, though, you're the one who's naked."

Startled, Arthur grabbed a towel and wrapped it around his waist as he tried to compose himself. Then he raised his voice.

"All right now, the joke's over, you can come out of there, go home, and tell Paul it was lame. Very, very lame."

She didn't know Paul, she told him. "And could you please stop yelling. Other people may not be able to hear me, but I can hear perfectly well."

Arthur was much too tired for this nonsense. This young woman seemed deeply disturbed. He had just finished moving in, and all he wanted was some peace and quiet. "Look, give me a break," he told the young woman. "Take your stuff and go on home. Come out of that closet, for God's sake!"

The young woman looked at him sadly. "I'm afraid it's not that easy. I haven't quite gotten the hang of it yet, though it's improved in the last few days."

"What's 'improved' in the last few days?"

"Shut your eyes, I'm going to try."

"To try what?"

"To get out of this closet. That's what you want, isn't it? So shut your eyes, I have to concentrate. And don't say anything for a couple of minutes."

"You're out of your tree!"

"Just shut up and close your eyes. That way we won't have to spend the night here."

Not knowing what else to do, Arthur obeyed. Two seconds later he heard a voice coming from the living room.

"Not bad. I missed the couch, but still, not bad at all."

He hurried from the bathroom and saw the young woman sitting on the floor in the middle of the living room. She acted as though nothing were out of the ordinary.

"I'm glad you've kept the rugs, but I can't stand that painting on the wall," she said, indicating his college attempt at abstract expressionism.

"I'll hang whatever painting I want, wherever I want. I don't know how you do this place-shifting business. And really, I don't care. I simply want to go to bed. So if you won't tell me who you are, fine. I don't need to know. But just go home!"

"I am home. Or at least, I was. It's all so confusing."

Arthur shook his head. "Listen, I've been renting this place for ten days. This is my home, not yours."

"Yes, I know, you're my postmortem tenant. If you think about it, it's really rather funny."

"Funny? What do you mean, 'postmortem tenant'? The owner of this apartment is a woman in her seventies and very much alive—or at least that's what the broker told me."

"She'd love to hear that," she said sarcastically. "She's only sixty-two, although she has aged a lot recently. She's my mother, and for the time being she's my legal guardian. I'm the owner."

"You have a legal guardian?"

"Yes. In my present condition, I'm having a tough time signing papers."

"Are you under hospital care?"

"That's putting it mildly."

"Well, they must be very worried about you. Which hospital is it? I'll drive you there."

"Hey, you don't think I'm some nutcase that just escaped from an asylum?"

"No, not—"

"Because first you called me a whore and now it's a nutcase. That's a bit much for a first meeting."

"Listen, I really don't care who you are: whore, nutcase, some kind of fugitive from *Bewitched*. I'm exhausted and I just want to go to bed and get some sleep."

She ignored him and kept on with her questions. "How do I seem to you?"

"Seem? Disturbed. You seem very disturbed," he said flatly.

"I mean physically. I can't see myself in mirrors. How do I look?"

Arthur hesitated before describing her. He told himself that maybe, if he went along with her charade for just a bit, he could get rid of her. And she really was quite striking, he realized as he concentrated on her appearance. "You're rather pretty," he admitted. "You're about average height, rather slender—long legs, I see. Your eyes—" he stopped short. Her eyes were remarkable—an indeterminate color that seemed to be every color at once, almost like the eyes of a newborn. But he wasn't going to get caught up in this folly. "You have a full mouth, pale skin, a pleasing face whose sweetness is in total contrast to your behavior. Your hair is a bit of a mess and could use a good combing out, but it's quite a nice color."

She laughed. "If I asked for directions to Market Street, would you list every building I'd pass on the way?"

"I'm sorry, I don't get the joke."

"Do you always describe women so minutely?"

Arthur felt his anger rising. He was fed up. "How did you get in here? Do you have copies of the keys?"

"I don't need keys. It's so amazing that you can see me. A miracle. I just can't get over it. And your description of me was really very sweet." She patted the floor beside her. "Please sit down here beside me. What I have to tell you is not easy to understand. It may seem impossible to accept. But if you'll listen to my story—if you're willing to trust me—then maybe in the end you'll believe me. And it's very important that you, in particular, should believe me. For without knowing it, you're the only person in the world who can share my secret."

Arthur sighed. He would have to hear this young woman out. So even though all he wanted was sleep, he sat down next to her and listened to the most improbable tale he had ever heard.

Her name was Lauren Kline, and she claimed to be a doctor, a medical resident. She told him that she'd been in a car accident six months ago—a serious one—when her steering system failed. "I've been in a coma ever since. No, don't start thinking yet; just let me explain."

She had no memory of the accident. She'd regained consciousness in the recovery room. Overwhelmed by the strangest sensations, she found she could hear everything going on around her, but could neither move nor speak. At first she attributed this to the anesthesia she'd been under. "But I was wrong. Hours went by, days, and I couldn't physically wake up." It had been the most terrifying period of her life. For several days she'd been convinced she was quadriplegic. "You have no idea what I went through. A prisoner inside my body, for life."

She had wished with all her might to die, she said. "But it's hard to end it all when you can't even lift your little finger. My mother sat by my bed, and I begged her with my thoughts to smother me with a pillow." One day a doctor had walked in, and she had recognized his voice: it was her supervising physician, Alan Fernstein. Mrs. Kline had asked him whether her daughter could hear when people spoke to her. Fernstein had said he didn't know, but that studies suggested that comatose patients were sometimes aware of what went on around them. So they should all be careful what they said around Lauren.

"Mom asked him if there was any chance I'd come back one day." Fernstein had answered quietly that he still didn't know. However, he added, she could hold on to a reasonable measure of hope, because people had been known to emerge from comas even after several months—it was rare, but it happened. "Anything is possible," he'd said. "We're not gods; we don't know everything. Deep coma is a mystery to medicine."

"I was relieved to hear that," Lauren said. "My body was relatively undamaged. The diagnosis wasn't exactly comforting, but at least it wasn't definitive. Quadriplegia would have been irreversible. But with a coma, there is at least *some* hope—no matter how slim."

The weeks had dragged on—long, then even longer. Lauren had spent those weeks immobile, traveling through her memories. Then one night, hearing the bustle on the other side of her hospital-room door, she had pictured the corridor—the nurses scurrying by, arms full of folders or pushing carts, colleagues coming and going from one room to another.

"And that's the first time it happened: suddenly, there I

was, in the middle of the corridor I'd been visualizing so intently. At first I thought it was my imagination playing tricks. I know the place well; after all, I worked in that hospital. But it all felt so astoundingly real. I could actually see the staff around me: Betty opening the supply closet, taking out some compresses, and shutting it again; Bill going past scratching his head—it's a nervous tic of his, he does it all the time."

She had heard the elevator doors, smelled the meals being served. No one had seen her. People walked right by her without even trying to avoid her—completely unaware of her presence. After a while, exhausted, she had returned to her body.

Over the next few days Lauren had learned how to move around inside the hospital. She would concentrate on imagining the cafeteria and find herself inside it; or the emergency room, and presto, there she was. After three months of practice she found she could leave the confines of the hospital. She had shared a meal with a French couple at one of her favorite restaurants, watched half a movie at the local cinema, and spent several hours in her mother's apartment. "I didn't repeat that visit. It hurt too much to be beside her without being able to communicate." Kali had sensed her presence and gone crazy, racing around in circles, whimpering. So Lauren had returned to her apartment. It was, after all, her home, and it was still the place she felt most at ease.

"I live completely alone. You can't imagine what it's like, not to be able to talk to anyone—to be totally transparent, not to exist in anyone's life. That's why I was so blown away when you spoke to me this evening, and I realized you could see me. I don't know why, but I only hope it lasts. I could talk to you for hours; I so badly need to talk. I've seen so much, thought so much, been so alone for so long. I've stored up so many things to say." Her rush of words gave way to a moment of silence. Tears welled up in her eyes. She looked at Arthur. Her hand reached out and touched his arm. "You must think I'm crazy?"

Arthur's annoyance had left him. Despite himself, he was moved by the young woman's emotion and mesmerized by her story.

"No, you don't seem crazy. But this is all very—I don't even know how to put it—disturbing, surprising, extraordinary. I don't know what to say. I'd like to help you, but I don't know how I can."

"Let me stay here. I won't bother you."

"You truly believe everything you just told me?"

"You didn't believe a word I said?" Her face fell. "You think I'm some weirdo who's just landed on you? I guess I never stood a chance, did I?"

Arthur asked her to put herself in his place. How would she react if, in the middle of the night, she found a man hiding in her bathroom closet—a somewhat overwrought man, hell-bent on explaining that he was some kind of ghost whose body was lying somewhere else in a coma. Lauren's features relaxed, and she smiled a little. She had to admit that her first reaction would be to scream. She granted him that the circumstances were bizarre.

"But I beg you, Arthur, you must believe me. Nobody could make up a story like this."

"You're wrong there—my business partner could easily dream up a practical joke on this scale."

"Forget your partner, Arthur. He has nothing to do with it. This isn't a joke."

"How do you know my name?"

"Oh, I was here when you looked over the apartment with the Realtor. I was flattered you liked it so much. I remember you signed the lease on the kitchen counter. I was also here when you brought up your boxes and you broke your model airplane." She giggled. "Of course, I'm sorry you broke your toy, but, oh, the cursing and shouting. I even watched you hang that hideous painting on the wall, although I admit I used all my willpower trying to make it fall down.

"I was here when you did your obsessive-compulsive number with the drafting table. You must have shifted it twenty times before putting it in the only position it could possibly fit. It was so obvious, I couldn't figure out why it took you so long.

"I've been with you since the first day. The whole time."

"You're here when I take a shower and when I'm in bed?"

"Don't worry. I'm not a voyeur. Although I must say you're quite nicely built. Apart from those love handles—you'll need to keep an eye on those—but aside from that, you're really quite attractive."

Arthur frowned. She was convincing—or rather, had certainly convinced herself—but her story just didn't make sense. If she wanted to believe it, let her. He had no reason to attempt to persuade her she was deluded; he wasn't her therapist, after all. He glanced at the clock. He just wanted to sleep, and she seemed harmless enough. So, to bring things to a halt, he offered to put her up for the night. He would take the couch in the living room, "the one below my hideous attempt at art," and she could take his bedroom. Tomorrow she would go back to wherever she'd come from—back to the hospital, or wherever else she wanted to go—and that would be the end of it.

But Lauren disagreed. She stood squarely in front of him, her face defiant, determined. Taking a deep breath, she reeled off an astonishing list of all he had said and done in the last few days. She repeated his phone conversation with Carol Ann last Saturday. "She hung up on you right after you lectured her, fairly pompously I must say, about the reasons you don't want to discuss your relationship anymore. *Believe me!*" She reminded him of the two cups he had broken unpacking. *"Believe me!"* And of how he had overslept and scalded himself in the shower. *"Believe me!"* She teased him about the time he had spent looking for his keys, and the tantrum he'd thrown. (Incidentally, she did find him rather inattentive—the keys had been right there, in plain sight, all along, on the little table by the front door.) *"For heaven's sake, do believe me."* The phone company had come on Tuesday at five after keeping him waiting for three hours. He had eaten a pastrami sandwich, spilled mustard on his coat, and had to change before going out again. "Now do you believe me?"

"So you've been spying on me for days. Why?"

"How the heck could I be spying on you? This isn't the Watergate building. Can you see any cameras or microphones?"

"No, I can't, but it would make more sense than your story."

"Get your car keys!" she ordered.

"And where are we going?"

"To the hospital. I'll take you to see me."

"Oh, sure. It's the middle of the night and I'm supposed to schlepp over to a hospital on the other side of town and ask the night nurses to please conduct me to the room of a woman I don't know, because her ghost is in my apartment, and I really want to get some sleep, but she's dug her heels in, and this is the only way I can get her to leave me in peace."

"Do you know of any other?"

"Any other what?"

"Any other way you'll get some sleep."

"Dear God, what did I do to deserve this?"

"You don't believe in God. You said so on the phone to your business partner: 'Paul, I don't believe in God. If we get this contract, it's because we're the best. If we lose it, we'll have to ask ourselves where we went wrong.' Well, consider just for a moment that you might be wrong now. That's all I ask. Believe me! I need you. You're my only hope!"

Hearing Lauren mention Paul's name prompted Arthur to pick up the phone and dial his partner's number.

"Paul, did I wake you?"

Paul's voice was groggy. "No, no, it's one in the morning and I was waiting for your bedtime call before going to sleep."

"Really? Was I supposed to call you?"

"No, you weren't supposed to call me, and yes, you did wake me up. What do you want?"

"To hand the phone over to someone and let you know that this time your stupid jokes have gone too far."

Arthur handed the phone to Lauren and asked her to speak to his partner. She couldn't take the phone—she explained she couldn't hold on to anything solid. By now somewhat irritated, Paul asked Arthur who he was talking to. Arthur smiled in triumph and pressed the button for the speakerphone.

"Can you hear me, Paul?"

"Yes, I can hear you. What is this about? I'd like to get back to sleep."

"I'd like to sleep too, so shut up for a minute. Speak to him, Lauren—go ahead, talk!"

She shrugged.

"If you like. Hello, Paul. You most certainly can't hear me. Unlike your partner, who can hear me, but won't listen to me."

"Okay, Arthur, that's enough. If you don't have anything to say, it's really late."

"Answer her."

"Answer who?"

"The person who just spoke to you."

"You're the person who just spoke to me, and I'm answering."

"You didn't hear anyone else talking?"

"Are you hallucinating? What are you, Joan of Arc?"

Lauren was staring pityingly at Arthur. Arthur shook his head. If these two had planned this thing for a joke, Paul would not have strung it out for so long. This wasn't his style. He told Paul to forget it and apologized for calling so late. Apparently genuinely anxious, Paul asked if everything was all right, or if he should come over.

Arthur reassured him, "Everything's fine. Forget it. Thanks."

"No need to thank me, buddy. If you have a problem, you can wake me anytime with this kind of crap, be my guest! We're partners for better or worse, so whenever you're having a bad patch, you wake me up and we'll share. Okay, can I go back to sleep or do you have anything else on your mind?"

"Good night, Paul."

They hung up.

"Take me to the hospital. We could have been there by now."

"No, I won't take you to the hospital. If I take one step out this door, I'm already halfway to accepting your crazy story. I'm tired and I want to go to bed. So you take my bedroom and I'll take the couch, or else you can leave. That's my last offer."

"You're even more stubborn than I am. Keep your room, I don't need a bed."

"And what will you do?"

"Does it matter?"

"It matters."

"I'll stay right here in the living room."

"Until tomorrow morning. But after that . . ."

"Yes, until tomorrow morning. Thanks so much for the gracious hospitality."

"And no spying in my bedroom!"

"Since you think I'm faking, just lock your door, and if you're worried about it because you sleep naked, I've already seen you, you know."

"I thought you weren't a voyeur."

She pointed out that when he'd opened the closet, a while ago, she would have had to be blind not to notice he had no clothes on. He cringed and wished her good night. "You, too, Arthur, and sleep well."

Arthur slammed the door to his bedroom. "She's mad," he grumbled. "This is insane." He fell into bed. The green numerals of his radio alarm blinked 1:30. He watched them blink until 2:11, then leaped up, pulled on a thick sweater, jeans, and socks, and strode into the living room. Lauren was sitting cross-legged on the window seat. When he came in, she spoke to him without turning around.

"I love this view, don't you? It's what convinced me to buy this apartment. I love looking at the bridge lit up at night. In the summer I like to open the window and hear the foghorns when the cargoes go out to sea. I always tried to count how many waves the ships would break through before they passed under the Golden Gate."

"All right, let's go."

"Really? What changed your mind?"

"You've already destroyed most of my night, and I may as well settle this right now. I'm supposed to work tomorrow. I have an important lunch meeting, and I really need at least two hours' sleep. So hurry up here."

"Go ahead, I'll join you."

"What do you mean, you'll join me? Where?"

"I said I'll join you. Trust me for just two minutes."

Under the circumstances Arthur felt that he had already trusted her quite sufficiently. Before leaving, he asked her again for her last name. She gave it to him, along with the room number where she was supposedly hospitalized: Room 505. Easy to remember. He saw nothing easy in what lay ahead. He locked the door behind him and went down the stairs into the garage. Lauren was already sitting in the backseat of his car.

"I don't know how you did that, but I'm very impressed. You must have worked with Houdini."

"Who?"

"Houdini, the escape artist. Come sit up front; I'm not in the mood to play chauffeur."

"Can you try to go a little easy on me? I told you, I don't have this thing down yet. The backseat is pretty good—I could have landed on the roof. Trust me, I'm improving."

Lauren clambered over to sit next to him. She looked out the window in silence as Arthur drove through the night. He broke the silence to ask her what he should say once they reached the hospital.

She had an idea. "You're my cousin from Argentina. You've just heard the news, and you've driven through the night to get here. Your flight to England leaves at dawn and you won't be back for six months. So they just have to break the rules and let you visit your beloved cousin, even though it's late."

Arthur didn't think he made a convincing Argentinean and predicted that the ruse would fail. She told him not to be so negative. "Stop worrying," she said. "If worst comes to worse, we'll come back tomorrow." Arthur was more worried about this woman's wild imagination. Just then, the Saab turned into the hospital complex. She told him to make a right, then take the second lane to his left and park just beyond the silver pine. Once they'd parked, she pointed out the night bell, warning him not to ring it too long because it annoyed them. "Who?" he asked.

"The nurses. They have to come from the far end of a long hall, and they don't know how to teleport. So come on, wake up."

"I only wish I could."

Chapter
FIVE

*A*rthur stepped up to the night buzzer and gave it two short rings. A small woman with round tortoiseshell glasses opened the door and asked what he wanted. He stumbled through Lauren's preposterous story as best he could. The nurse told him that the hospital had rules, the rules were meant to be followed, and he should just postpone his flight and come back to the hospital in the morning.

He begged. He invoked the importance of family and the exception that just proves the rule. Nothing worked, and he was about to acknowledge defeat when he saw the nurse weaken. She glanced at her watch and said, "I have to do my rounds. Follow me, don't make a sound, don't touch anything, and in fifteen minutes you're out of here."

He took her hand and kissed it to show his gratitude. "Are you all like that in Argentina?" she asked with a slight smile. She opened the door wider to allow him inside. They walked to the elevators and went straight up to the fifth floor.

"I'll take you to her room, I'll do my rounds, and I'll come back to get you. Don't touch anything."

She opened the door to Room 505. The room was dark, lit only by a small yellow night-light. From the doorway, Arthur could see a woman lying on the bed, apparently sleeping deeply; he could not make out her features.

The nurse spoke in a whisper. "I'll leave the door open—go on in, there's no chance she'll wake up, but be careful what you say, you never know with coma patients. At least, that's what the doctors say."

Arthur hovered near the doorway. Lauren was standing by the window and urged him into the room. "Go on, I'm not going to bite you." He couldn't stop wondering what the hell he was doing there. He went up to the bed. The resemblance was striking. The motionless woman was paler than her double, smiling at him from the windowsill, and thinner, but their features were identical.

He took a step back. "Are you twins?"

"You're hopeless. I don't have a sister. That's me lying there, just me. No one is playing tricks on you and you aren't dreaming. Arthur, please, you're the only chance I have, don't turn your back on me. I need your help. You're the only person I've been able to communicate with in the past six months—the only human being who sees me and hears me."

"Why me?"

"I haven't the slightest idea. Maybe because of the apartment? But there's no logic to all this."

"It's scary."

"Don't you think I'm frightened too?"

She was frightened. It was her body that frightened her, drying up little by little, every day, like a vegetable on a shelf: lying there motionless, with an IV drip to irrigate her, a feeding tube to nourish her, and a catheter to carry away her waste. She had no answers to Arthur's questions. They were the same questions she'd been asking herself every day since the accident. "You can't even begin to imagine what goes through my mind." Her eyes cloudy, she told him about her doubts and worries. How long would this mysterious situation continue? Would she ever come back to life, even just for a few days, to lead a normal life again, walk on two legs, and hold the people she cared for in her arms? Why had she spent those years studying medicine if she was only going to end like this? How many more days did she have before her heart gave out? She was watching herself die, and she was terrified. "Arthur, what I am is a living ghost." He dropped his eyes from hers.

"You're not dead, you're right here. Come on, we're going home. I'm tired and so are you. I'll drive you back."

He put his arm across her shoulders and pulled her toward him comfortingly. Turning around, he found himself face-to-face with the nurse, who was looking at him with dismay.

"Are you okay?"

"Yes, why?"

"Your arm in the air like that, with your fingers curled— it looks like you have some sort of cramp."

Arthur hurriedly removed his hand from Lauren's shoulder and let his arm fall by his side. "You can't see her, can you?"

"Can't see who?"

"Nobody."

"Would you like to rest a little before you leave? All of a sudden you seem a little overwrought." The nurse tried to soothe him: it was always a shock, "it's completely normal," it would pass. Arthur spoke slowly, as if searching for his words: "No, really, I'm fine. I'll just go now." She worried that he might not be able to find his way back out of the building. Pulling himself together, Arthur reassured her that he could: the exit was just at the end of the hall.

"I'll leave you here then. I've still got to change the sheets on the bed next door."

Arthur said good-bye and started down the corridor. The nurse saw him lift his arm back to the horizontal and heard him mumble, "I believe you, Lauren, I believe you." The nurse frowned and went into the next room. "Some people get so shaken up, there's just nothing you can say."

Arthur and Lauren headed out of the hospital together in silence. A north wind had blown in from the ocean, bringing with it drizzling rain. It was suddenly quite cold. Arthur pulled his coat collar up and opened the car door for Lauren. "We're going to have to lighten up a little on the walking-through-walls act. Do you mind?"

She climbed into the car in the conventional manner and smiled.

Neither uttered a word on the way back. Arthur concentrated on the road, trying to keep at bay the thousands of questions that were flooding his mind, while Lauren watched the clouds scudding over the night sky. Only when they were nearly home did she speak, without turning her face from the window.

"I used to love the night for its silence, all those shapes without shadows, the looks of strangers you never catch during the daytime. It's as if two separate worlds share the same city without knowing each other, without imagining that the other world even exists. So many people appear in the evening and disappear with the dawn. No one knows where they go. The hospital personnel, the late-night workers—we're the only ones who really know them."

"Lauren, you've got to admit this all seems impossible."

"Yes, but please let's not spend the rest of the night discussing it."

"You mean what's left of my night."

Arthur parked the car on the street to avoid waking his neighbors with the noise of the garage door. Slowly, he went upstairs and into his apartment. Lauren was already sitting cross-legged in the middle of the living room.

"Did you aim for the couch?" he asked, amused.

"No, I aimed for the carpet and landed right on target."

"You're bluffing, I bet you aimed for the couch."

"And I'm telling you I aimed for the rug!"

"Liar."

"I would love to be able to make you some tea. But you should go on to bed."

Arthur questioned her about her accident. She told him about her Triumph's last caprice. About how much she'd loved that car, and the weekend trip to Carmel that she'd planned to take early the previous summer, and how it had all ended on Union Square. She couldn't recall the exact details.

"And your boyfriend?"

"What about my boyfriend?"

"Were you planning to meet him?"

Lauren smiled. "What you mean is, do I have a boyfriend?"

"So, did you have a boyfriend?"

"I love that past tense—yes, I did sometimes."

"You haven't answered the question."

"Is it any of your business?"

"You're right, it isn't."

Arthur turned toward the bedroom, again offering Lauren the bed. "Really, I don't mind sleeping on the couch," he assured her. She thanked him for his gallantry, but the couch was fine. He went to bed too tired to think about all of the evening's implications; there would be time for that tomorrow. Before he closed the door he wished her good night, and she asked him one last favor.

"Would you mind giving me a hug?" Arthur cocked his head coyly. "It's been six months since anyone held me in their arms." He walked over, took her by the shoulders, and pulled her into the circle of his arms. She rested her head against his chest. They stood like that for a few minutes. Arthur felt awkward, at a loss. She felt fragile and a bit cold, but she felt real. Clumsily, he dropped his hands to her slender waist. She brushed his shoulder with her cheek.

"Thank you, Arthur, thank you for everything. Go to sleep now; you must be exhausted. I'll wake you at eight."

He went to his bedroom, peeled off sweater and shirt, tossed his pants on a chair, and crawled under the covers. Moments later he was asleep.

Lauren remained in the living room until she could safely assume he was sleeping, then shut her eyes, concentrated, and made a wobbly landing on the arm of the big chair facing the bed. She watched him as he slept. Arthur's face looked peaceful; she could even see the beginnings of a smile at the corners of his mouth. How good it was to connect with another human being. She gazed at him until slumber overwhelmed her, too. It was the first time she had managed to sleep since the accident.

. . .

*W*hen Lauren awoke, it was ten o'clock; Arthur was still fast asleep. "Oh my God!" she said loudly, and sat down beside the bed, shaking him vigorously. "Wake up!"

He turned over, protesting. "Take it easy, Carol Ann."

"Charming, absolutely charming. Wake up. This isn't Carol Ann, and it's already past ten."

At first Arthur's eyelids parted slowly; then they snapped wide open and he jolted upright.

"You're disappointed? You'd prefer Carol Ann?"

"It's you. So it wasn't a dream?"

"You could have spared me that line, it's awfully predictable. Come on. You'd better hurry, you're late for work."

"What? You were supposed to wake me," he yelled.

"It's okay, I'm not deaf—was Carol Ann? I'm sorry; I fell asleep, which hasn't happened to me since the accident. I was hoping we could celebrate, but obviously you're not in the mood."

"Don't use that sarcastic tone with me. You kept me up all night, and now I'm going to be late. If you'd be so kind . . ."

"You're so gracious in the morning. I think I like you better asleep."

"You're not going to make a scene, are you?"

"Don't even think about it. Go on, get dressed, or it will be my fault again."

"Of course it's your fault. Now, would you mind leaving the room so I can have a little privacy?"

"So all of a sudden you're a prude?"

He told her to spare him the household drama and was foolhardy enough to finish his sentence with "or else."

"That's two words too many," she shot back. She coldly wished him a good day, and vanished.

Arthur looked all around, hesitated for a moment, then called out, "Lauren? I know you're here somewhere. Come on out, this is ridiculous." As he stood there in his boxers, waving his arms about, he caught the eye of his neighbor across the street, who was watching the scene from his window with an air of astonishment. Arthur grabbed a blanket, wrapped it around his waist, and headed for the bathroom, muttering, "I never get to work this late, I'm half-naked in the middle of my room, I'm talking to a ghost—how the hell did all this happen to me?"

In the bathroom he opened the closet door and asked softly, "Lauren, are you there?" Again there was no reply, and he was disappointed. He showered at top speed. When he finished, he returned to the bedroom, checked for Lauren in the other closet, and, not finding her, put on his suit. To his fury, it took him three attempts before he could knot his tie. Once dressed, he went to the kitchen, scrabbled through the drawer for his keys, but finally found them in his pocket. He hurried from the apartment, stopped in his tracks, turned, and opened the door again. "Lauren, still not there?" After a few seconds' silence, he double-locked the door. Taking the outside stairs straight to the garage, he looked for his car. Remembering that he had parked it in the street, he ran back down the hallway and finally reached the sidewalk. Raising his eyes, he saw his neighbor again, staring at him with a puzzled look. He gave him an embarrassed smile, fumbled with the key as he unlocked the car door, sat behind the wheel, and roared away.

. . .

*W*hen Arthur reached the office, Paul was standing in the reception area, clad, as always, in black from head to toe. He shook his head several times when he caught sight of Arthur and, with a wry expression on his face, said, "Maybe you should take a few days off."

"Eat it. Don't piss me off this morning, Paul."

"Charming—absolutely charming."

"What is it with everyone this morning? Don't *you* get at me too."

"You've seen Carol Ann again?"

"No, I haven't seen Carol Ann. It's over with Carol Ann, and you know it."

"There are only two explanations for the state you're in: Carol Ann or a new one."

"There isn't a new one either. Now move, I'm late enough already."

"No kidding. After all, it's only a quarter of eleven. What's her name?"

"Whose?"

"Have you seen your face this morning?"

"What's the matter with it?"

"Come on. How was it? Tell me."

"I have nothing to tell."

"What about your late-night phone call with all that bullshit—what was that about?"

Arthur stared at his partner. "Look, I ate some bad seafood last night, and then I had a nightmare. I got very little sleep. Please, I'm really not in the mood. Let me get by—I'm late."

Paul moved aside. As Arthur passed him, Paul patted his

shoulder. "I'm your friend, aren't I?" Arthur turned, and Paul added, "You'd tell me if you were in trouble?"

"I slept badly last night, that's all. Don't make a thing out of it."

"Fine, fine. Lunch is at one, we're meeting at the top of the Hyatt Embarcadero. We can go together if you like. I'm coming back to the office afterward."

"No, I'll take my car. I have another meeting this afternoon."

"Whatever."

Arthur entered his office, put his briefcase on the desk, sat down, called his secretary, asked her for coffee, swiveled his chair around to face the window, leaned backward, and tried to think.

A few moments later Maureen tapped on the door. She carried a thick folder in one hand and a cup of coffee with a doughnut balanced on the edge of the saucer in the other. She set the cup and saucer on a corner of the desk and sat in the chair next to it.

"I put milk in it. I imagine it's your first of the day."

"Thanks." He paused for a second. "Uh, Maureen, do I look that bad?"

"You've got a 'Haven't had my first coffee yet' look."

"I haven't had my first coffee yet!"

"Okay, relax. Take your time. You have a bunch of messages, but there's nothing urgent, just these letters to be signed." She paused and eyed him suspiciously. "Are you okay?"

"Yes, a bit tired, that's all."

At that precise moment, Lauren materialized in the room. Narrowly missing the corner of the desk, she disappeared from Arthur's line of sight, falling on the rug beyond his desk. He leaped to his feet.

"Did you hurt yourself?"

"No, no, I'm okay," said Lauren.

"Why would I have hurt myself?" asked Maureen.

"Not you," Arthur said.

Maureen glanced around the room. "There aren't that many of us here."

"I was thinking out loud."

"You were thinking out loud that I'd hurt myself?"

"No, I was thinking about someone else, and I said my thoughts out loud. Doesn't that ever happen to you?"

Lauren, now sitting with legs crossed on the edge of the desk, decided to goad Arthur a little. "You didn't have to compare me to a nightmare when you were talking to Paul just now."

"I never called you a nightmare."

"I'm very glad to hear it," said Maureen. "How many nightmares bring you a cup of coffee in the morning?"

"Maureen, I'm not talking to you!"

"Then either there's a ghost in the room or else I've gone partially blind and I'm missing something. Which is it?"

"I'm sorry. It's ridiculous. I'm ridiculous. I'm exhausted and I'm thinking out loud. My mind's a million miles away."

"You've been working too hard, Arthur. Have you ever heard of burnout? You have to act at the first signs or it can take months to recover."

"Maureen, I'm not suffering from burnout. I just had a bad night, that's all."

Lauren broke in, "There you go again. Bad night. Nightmare."

"Stop it, please. I have to concentrate. Just be quiet for a few minutes."

"But I didn't say anything!" Maureen exclaimed.

"Maureen, please go back to your desk. I have to pull myself together. I'll do some breathing exercises, some relaxation exercises, and I'll be fine."

"Relaxation exercises? You're scaring me, Arthur, you really are."

"There's no reason to be scared. I'm fine. Now, just leave me alone—and hold all my calls. I just need a bit of peace and quiet."

Maureen reluctantly left the room, closing the door behind her. Spotting Paul in the corridor, she asked him to have a word with her, in private.

Alone in his office, Arthur stared at Lauren. "You've got to cut the *Bewitched* act, Lauren. You're putting me in an impossible position."

"I wanted to apologize for this morning. I shouldn't have gone off in a huff like that. I know how hard it is for you to deal with all this."

"I'm sorry; I was the one in a lousy mood. It's just been a lot to take in a very short time."

"Let's not spend the morning trading apologies. I wanted to talk to you."

Paul opened the door without knocking. "Can I have a word with you?"

"You are already, aren't you?"

"I've just spoken with Maureen; Arthur, what's going on with you?"

"Nothing. Just because I'm tired and arrived late for once doesn't mean I'm having a nervous breakdown."

"I didn't say you were having a breakdown."

"No, but that's what Maureen suggested. Apparently I look like a zombie this morning."

"Putting it mildly. Jesus, you really look like you had a rough night."

"It was a bit wild," Arthur admitted, trying to decide how much to tell Paul.

"I knew it! I knew there must be a woman involved in all this."

Arthur nodded, raising his brows.

"Aha! You see, you can't keep anything from me. I was sure! Anyone I know?"

"No, no way."

"Tell me about her. Who is she? When do I get to meet her?"

"It'll be tricky, Paul. I know this sounds strange, but she's kind of a ghost. My apartment is haunted. I found out by accident last night. She was living in my bathroom closet. I spent the night with her, but it was all very innocent. She's pretty, as ghosts go, not—" Arthur hunched his shoulders, imitating a monster. "Really, she's very pretty for someone who's come back from the dead—though in fact she hasn't really returned from the dead, she never completely died. So that explains it. Are things clearer now?"

Paul looked sympathetically at his partner. "Right. Look, Arthur, I think you need to see a doctor."

"Stop it, Paul, I'm absolutely fine." Arthur turned to Lauren. "You see, this isn't going to be easy."

"What's not going to be easy?" asked Paul.

"I wasn't talking to you."

"You were talking to the ghost? Is it here in the room?"

Arthur reminded him that "it" was a she, adding that she was sitting next to Arthur on the edge of the desk. Paul looked doubtfully at him and slowly ran the palm of his hand across his partner's desk.

"Listen, I know I sometimes go a bit far with my practical jokes, but this time, Arthur, you've gone completely overboard. You're scaring me. You can't see yourself, but you look as if you're at the end of your rope this morning."

"I'm tired, I barely slept. I'm sure I look awful, but inside I'm in great shape. I promise you, everything's just fine."

"You're in great shape inside? Well, the outside of you seems in pretty bad shape."

"Paul, let me get on with my work. You're my friend, not my therapist; in fact, I don't even have a therapist. I don't need one."

Paul asked him not to come to their one o'clock signature meeting on the Swope deal. If he did, he might lose them the contract. "I don't believe you realize what kind of state you're in. You're pretty scary."

Irritated, Arthur rose, picked up his briefcase, and walked to the door.

"Okay, I'm scary. I look insane. Fine, I'll go home. Get out of my way, Paul. Come on, Lauren, we're out of here!"

"Brilliant, Arthur. You're a genius. That ghost number is fantastic."

"It's not a number, Paul. You're too—what's the word?—conventional to understand what I'm experiencing. But you'll notice that I don't hold it against you. I've come a long way myself since last night."

"Listen to yourself. It's mind-blowing!"

"Yes, so you've already said. Listen, don't worry about a thing. It's good that you offered to handle the meeting by yourself. I really didn't get much sleep, so I'm going to get some rest. Thanks. I'll be back tomorrow, and everything will be much better."

Paul suggested that Arthur take a few days off, at least until the end of the week. Moving was always stressful. Paul would be happy to help Arthur over the weekend, if he needed anything at all. Arthur thanked Paul with a tinge of sarcasm, then left the room and ran down the stairs. Stepping out onto the sidewalk, he looked around for Lauren.

"Are you there?"

Lauren appeared, sitting on the hood of his car. "I'm creating a whole load of problems for you. I'm really sorry."

"No, don't be. The fact is, I haven't done this for ages."

"Done what?"

"Skipped work. Just think, an entire day playing hooky!"

*S*tanding at the office window, brow creased, Paul watched his partner talk to himself in the street, open the passenger door for no reason and then close it again, walk around the car, and climb in behind the wheel. Arthur really must be going through some kind of breakdown.

Sitting in the driver's seat, Arthur put his hands on the wheel and sighed. He looked at Lauren and smiled, saying nothing.

A bit embarrassed, she returned his smile. "It's frustrating having someone think you're crazy, isn't it? At least he didn't call you a whore!"

"Why didn't he get it?" Arthur said facetiously. "Wasn't my explanation clear?"

"Clear as crystal. What now?"

"Breakfast, and then you can tell me everything, in detail."

Paul continued to watch his friend, parked below on the other side of the street. When he saw him talking to himself in the car, chatting with an invisible, imaginary friend, he decided to call him on his cell phone. When Arthur answered, Paul asked him not to start the car: he would be right down. They had to talk.

"What about?" asked Arthur.

"That's why I'm coming down!"

Paul ran downstairs, crossed the street, opened the driver's door, and almost sat on his best friend's lap.

"Move over!"

"Get in on the other side, for God's sake!"

"Do you mind if I do the driving?"

"I don't get it. Are we talking or going for a ride?"

"Both. Come on, change seats!"

Pushing Arthur over, Paul settled behind the wheel and turned the key. The car moved away from the curb. At the first intersection Paul braked hard.

"First things first: Is your ghost with us in the car right now?"

"Yes. She moved into the backseat after your cavalier entrance."

Paul opened his door, got out, tilted his seat forward, and said to Arthur, "Do me a favor. Ask Casper to get out of the car and leave us alone for a while. I have to have a private talk with you. You can catch up with each other at your place."

Lauren reappeared outside the passenger window. "Pick me up at North Point. I'll be taking a walk there. You know, if it's too complicated, you don't need to tell him the truth."

"He's my friend and my partner, I can't lie to him."

"Go ahead, discuss me with your glove compartment," said Paul. "Why, just last night I opened the refrigerator and saw a light inside, so I went in and talked about you with the butter and a head of lettuce for a good half hour."

"I'm not discussing you with the glove compartment. I'm talking to her."

"Well, then, please ask Lady Casper to go iron her sheet so that you and I can talk in peace."

Lauren vanished.

"Did it leave?" Paul asked a little anxiously.

"It's *she,* not *it*! Yes, she's gone. You're so rude. Now, what's up with you?"

"What's up with me?" repeated Paul, making a face. He turned the engine back on and headed down Sutter Street. "I just wanted to be alone so we could talk about something personal."

"Like what?"

"The delayed reactions that sometimes set in after people break up."

Paul launched into a long tirade. Carol Ann wasn't right for Arthur. In his view, she had hurt Arthur badly, and she wasn't worth it. When all was said and done, the woman was emotionally handicapped and didn't know how to be happy. Was she honestly worth what Arthur had gone through since their separation? He hadn't been wasted this way since Karen. Now Karen—she was a real loss, whereas, frankly, Carol Ann . . .

Arthur pointed out that he'd been only nineteen when Karen had broken it off; and, for the record, he added, he'd never hit on her. For almost fifteen years Paul had been bringing her up on the slimmest of pretexts, simply because he'd seen her first. Paul denied ever mentioning her. "At least two or three times a year!" Arthur retorted. "Presto, she pops out, a flash from the past. I can't even remember her face!"

Paul, suddenly annoyed, began to wave his arms. "Then why won't you tell me the truth about her? Admit it, for

God's sake, you went out with her! It's been fifteen years, like you said—the statute of limitations has expired!"

"You're getting on my nerves, Paul! You didn't come racing downstairs to drive halfway across town because all of a sudden you want to discuss Karen Lowenski! Where are we going, anyway?"

"You can't remember her face but you haven't forgotten her last name!"

"Is this the important personal matter you wanted to talk about?"

"No, I'm talking about Carol Ann."

"Why? I haven't seen her and we haven't talked on the phone. If that's what's worrying you, it's not worth driving to Los Angeles about—because, in case you haven't noticed, we're already south of Market. What's the matter with you? She invited you on a date, or something? What are you trying to tell me?"

"Nothing, I just want to talk. I want you to talk to me."

"About what?"

"About you."

*P*aul turned left and drove the Saab into the parking area of a big four-story building with a white-tiled facade.

"Paul, I know it'll seem crazy to you, but I really have met a ghost."

"Arthur, I know it'll seem crazy to you, but I really am taking you for a medical checkup."

Arthur, who had been looking at his friend, swiftly turned his head to stare at the name on the front of the building. "You're taking me to this clinic? Seriously? You don't believe me?"

"Of course I believe you! And I'll believe you even more when you've seen a doctor and had a brain scan."

"You want me to have a brain scan?"

"Listen to me, you big lug! If I arrive at the office one day looking like I've been stuck on an escalator for a month; and then I leave in a rage even though I never, ever lose my temper; and then you see me walk down the sidewalk with my elbow stuck way up in the air, and open my car door for a passenger who's not there; and then, as if that's not enough, I wave my hands around inside my car as if I'm talking to someone, but there's nobody else there, really no one—and all I can offer you by way of explanation is that I've just met a ghost—I hope you'll be as concerned for me as I am for you right now."

Arthur managed a smile. "When I met her in my closet, I thought it was one of your jokes."

"Come on, follow me, we're going to put my mind at rest now."

Arthur let himself be dragged by the arm to the clinic's reception area. The receptionist watched them as Paul sat Arthur on a chair and told him not to move. Paul was treating Arthur the way you treat an unruly child you don't want to let out of your sight. He walked to the desk and said urgently to the young woman, "This is an emergency!"

"What kind of emergency?" she asked, her voice distinctly casual, in contrast to Paul's impatience.

"The kind sitting in the chair, the one over there."

"No, I'm asking the nature of the emergency."

"Cranial shock."

"How did it happen?"

"Love is blind, and repeated blows on the head with a long white cane seem to have rattled his brain."

She found his answer droll, but wasn't sure she'd understood it fully. She was sorry, but with no appointment and no prescription, there was nothing she could do for him.

"We need to see Dr. Bresnick," Paul insisted.

"I'm sorry, but Dr. Bresnick is at the hospital today. I'll be happy to make you an appointment for tomorrow."

Paul was in no mood to pussyfoot around. He explained that all sixty partners in his powerful and prestigious architecture firm came annually to this clinic for their checkups. They all came right here to give birth, to get their kids vaccinated and their colds and bellyaches cared for. And every one of these nice, fat patients worked under his orders—his, and those of the man sitting in the waiting room with a vague look on his face.

"So, Miss, either Dr. Bresnick sees my partner this morning, or I guarantee that not one of my firm's employees will ever wipe his feet on your welcome mat again, not even to get a prescription for some Advil."

An hour later, still accompanied by Paul, Arthur found himself undressing for the first exam of a complete medical checkup. Following an electrocardiogram (he had to pedal a stationary bike for twenty minutes with electrodes stuck to his chest), a nurse took his blood (Paul couldn't stay in the room for that one) and performed a series of neurological tests (he had to lift one leg, with eyes open and eyes closed; his reflexes were tested on knees, elbows, and chin; a medic scratched the soles of his feet with a needle). Finally, under heavy pressure from Paul, the clinic agreed to perform a brain scan. The exam room was divided in two by a large glass screen. On one side lay a vast and impressive cylindrical machine, hollowed at the center to fit a patient's whole body. On the other side a series of screens and workstations were connected by a swarm of thick black cables. Arthur lay down, his head and hips strapped to a narrow platform covered in a white sheet. The medic pressed a button and the platform slid Arthur into the machine. His skin was only inches from the sides of the narrow cylinder; he couldn't move. He had been warned how claustrophobic he might feel in there.

He would be alone for the time it took to perform a scan, but he could communicate with Paul and the medic, on the other side of the glass divide, through a small microphone that had been installed inside the machine. The door closed and the huge cylinder commenced emitting a series of loud noises.

"Is he going through hell?" Paul asked, looking amused.

The medic explained that it was disagreeable. People who were claustrophobic hated it; they did sometimes freak out. "It doesn't hurt at all, but being shut in, with the noise, makes it hard to take."

"And you can see inside the brain?"

"Yep."

"What do you find?"

"Clots, tumors . . ."

The phone rang, and the medic picked up. After a few seconds' conversation, he told Paul he would have to go attend to something, just for a few minutes. Paul shouldn't touch anything; it was all automatic.

When the medic left, Paul stared at his friend through the glass, with a playful smile on his face. His eyes went to the button that controlled the microphone in Arthur's scanner. He hesitated, then pushed it.

"Arthur, it's me! The doc left—but don't worry, I have everything under control. It's amazing how many buttons there are on this thing. It's like being in the cockpit of an airplane. And I'm driving—the pilot just parachuted out! So tell me, pal, you'll give it to me straight now, won't you? You did sleep with Karen, didn't you?"

*W*hen they left the clinic, Arthur was holding a dozen or so large brown envelopes containing the results of the battery of tests he'd passed—all perfectly normal.

"Do you believe me now?" he asked.

"Drop me off at the office and go home and rest, like you said."

"You're avoiding my question. Do you believe me, now you know I don't have a brain tumor?"

"Listen, go rest, it's probably just stress."

"Paul, I played fair and did the checkup you wanted, now you play fair too!"

"This isn't a fun game. We'll talk about it later. I'll get a taxi to the meeting. I'll phone you at home afterward."

Paul left Arthur alone in his Saab. Arthur had to admit, deep inside, he was beginning to enjoy this whole wacky story—its heroine, and the crazy situations it was bound to provoke. He drove toward North Point.

Chapter
SIX

*T*he Sea-View restaurant perched on a cliff overlooking the Pacific. Its dining area was almost full. Two TV screens over the bar allowed patrons to watch two different football games at once. The bets were rolling. Lauren and Arthur sat behind a glass bay window.

Arthur was about to order a glass of white wine when he was startled by a tickling sensation. Lauren was stroking his leg with her bare foot, eyes full of mischief and a triumphant smile on her face. Responding in kind, he grabbed her ankle and ran his hand up the length of her leg.

"I can feel you, too!" he exclaimed.

"I wanted to be sure."

"You are now."

The waitress looked dubiously at him. "What can you feel?"

"Nothing. I don't feel anything."

"You just said, 'I can feel you, too.' "

He turned to Lauren, who was now smiling broadly. "I could get myself locked up for this."

"Maybe that's not such a bad idea," said the waitress, turning on her heel.

"Hey, can you take my order?" he yelled after her.

"I'll send over Bob. We'll see if you can feel him, too."

Bob, if anything more feminine than his colleague, appeared a few minutes later. Arthur ordered scrambled eggs with salmon and a Virgin Mary. This time he waited for the server to leave before he spoke to Lauren. "Now, tell me everything again, from the beginning."

Bob halted in the middle of the room, looking askance as his customer started talking to the empty seat across from him. Lauren cut Arthur off in midsentence to ask if he had a cell phone. He didn't get what she had in mind, but nodded anyway.

"Take it out and pretend to be speaking into it; otherwise they really will lock you up."

Arthur looked around and realized that people at several tables had stopped eating and were staring at him, disconcerted by this person chatting alone. He grabbed his phone, punched in a number, and said, "Hello!" very loud. People went on staring at him for a few seconds, but once everything seemed more or less normal, they resumed their meals. He asked his question again into the mouthpiece.

"When this began," she told him, "when I realized I could move around in space, transparency was rather fun. It gave me a feeling of absolute freedom. No more worries about how to dress, or fixing my hair, or anything about how I looked: nobody saw me anymore. No more obligations, no more routine, and no more waiting in line. And your favorite part," she said with a playful smile—"I didn't have to respect anyone's privacy: I could eavesdrop on conversations, see the invisible, hear the inaudible, go where I had no right to be."

Bob arrived with the meal and set it before Arthur, all the while looking at him as if he were about to spring up and do something loony. Arthur ate with one hand, phone pressed to his ear with the other as he listened.

"I can go and sit in a corner of the Oval Office and listen to state secrets. I can sit on Richard Gere's lap or take a shower with Tom Cruise."

Everything, or almost everything, was possible to her. She could visit museums and boutiques when they were closed, enter a movie theater without paying, sleep in palaces, go for a spin in a fighter plane, observe the most advanced surgery, secretly visit research labs, or climb to the top of the Golden Gate Bridge. Arthur, ear glued to his cell phone, was curious to know whether she had tried at least one of those experiences.

"No, except for movies. I suffer from vertigo; I hate planes. Washington, D.C.'s too far, and I don't yet know how to transport myself long distances. As for sleeping in palaces, yesterday was the first time I've slept since this happened. And in the end, what's the point of shopping when you can't touch anything?"

"What about Richard Gere and Tom Cruise?"

"Same thing as shopping . . ." She smiled.

She told him with great earnestness that it was no fun at all being a ghost. In fact, she was miserable. Everything was within her reach but impossible to grasp. She missed her friends and the people she loved. "I can see them, but it hurts more than it helps. Maybe this is purgatory—to be eternally alone. I'm in limbo: not dead, not really alive."

"Do you believe in God?"

"Not really, but you tend to reevaluate these things in my condition. I didn't believe in ghosts, either."

"Neither do I," he said.

"You don't believe in ghosts?"

"You're not really a ghost."

"I'm not?"

"You're not dead, Lauren. Your heart is beating in one place, and your spirit is alive somewhere else. They've just separated, temporarily. We have to find out why, then try to bring them back together."

"You'll agree that it's a separation with awfully heavy consequences."

This was all way beyond his sphere of comprehension, but Arthur did not intend to leave it at that. His phone still pressed to his ear, he told her he wanted to learn more. They had to find a way to get her back into her body; otherwise she would never come out of her coma. The two things must be linked, he added.

"I believe you've made a breakthrough in your research, Doctor!"

He ignored her sarcasm and suggested that they go home and search the Web. He wanted to read every article pertaining to coma: scientific studies, medical reports, bibliographies, histories, eyewitness accounts. He was particularly interested in people who had come back after being in a long-term coma. "We have to track them down and question them. What they tell us could be very important."

"Why are you doing this?" She was looking at him skeptically.

"Because you sure can't."

"Answer my question. Do you realize what this will mean for you? How long it will take? You have your job, your own obligations."

"First you want my help, then you don't. You're a woman of contradictions."

"No, I just see things more clearly now. Didn't you notice that people were looking at you like you were crazy because you were alone at this table talking to yourself? Do you realize that next time you come to this restaurant they'll tell you they're full?"

"This city has more than a thousand restaurants. There are tons of them left."

"Arthur, you're very kind, really very kind, but you're being unrealistic."

"I don't mean to hurt your feelings, but you're hardly in a position to accuse someone else of being unreal."

"Don't play with my words, Arthur. . . . And don't make these wild promises to me. You'll never be able to figure this out. The truth is you just won't have time."

"I hate doing this in a restaurant, but you give me no choice. Excuse me a second."

Arthur pretended to hang up, looked into her eyes, picked up the phone again, and called his partner's number. He thanked Paul for his concern and for the time he had spent with him that morning. He had given it a lot of thought and concluded that Paul was right. He was indeed on the brink of a nervous breakdown brought on by overwork, and it would be best for the firm and for himself if he took some time off. He would phone in to deal with anything major, and Maureen would help. He was far too exhausted to go away anyway. He would be at home and could be reached by phone.

"There," he said as he clicked off the phone. "I'm now free of all professional obligations, and I suggest we begin our research at once."

"I don't know what to say."

"Start off by helping me get a grip on the medical aspects."

Bob arrived with the check, watching Arthur warily. Arthur popped his eyes wide open, made a frightening face, stuck his tongue out, and sprang to his feet. Bob took a step back.

"I expected better of you, Bob. I'm very disappointed. Come, Lauren, this place is unworthy of us."

Driving back to the apartment, Arthur outlined the methods he intended to use in his investigation. They exchanged ideas and agreed on a plan of action.

Chapter
SEVEN

*B*ack at home, Arthur sat down at his desk. He turned on his computer and logged on to the Internet. The information superhighway gave him instant access to hundreds of databases. He clicked on a search engine, then typed the word *coma* in the appropriate box. His search yielded several sites containing articles, first-person accounts, and analyses. There were even newsgroups with person-to-person exchanges on the subject. Lauren settled onto the corner of the desk so she could read everything along with him.

Their first step was to link up to Memorial Hospital's web page, where they selected the heading "Neuropathology and Cerebral Traumatology." This led them to a recent article on cranial trauma by a Dr. Silverstone. In it, he explained the classification of the different degrees of consciousness according to the Glasgow Scale. A series of three digits indicated the degree to which patients reacted to visual, auditory, and sensory stimuli. The digits corresponding to Lauren's case were 1.1.2, which added up to a class-four coma, otherwise known as "irreversible coma." Arthur then accessed a statistical analysis of patient outcomes in each class of coma. No one had ever returned from a voyage in "fourth class."

A number of diagrams, cross-sections of nerves, drawings, case histories, treatment protocols, and bibliographical sources were downloaded into Arthur's computer, then printed. All told, nearly seven hundred pages of information sorted and classified by topic.

Arthur ordered a pizza and two beers and announced that there was nothing left to do but read. Again, Lauren asked him why he was doing all this. He answered, "Out of a sense of duty, for someone who has given me a great deal in very little time, the most important thing of all being a new taste of excitement and wonder. You know, all dreams have a price." Then he went back to his reading, making marginal notes beside passages he didn't understand, which was almost all of them. As they went along, Lauren explained the terminology and medical theories.

Arthur pinned a large sheet of paper to his drafting table and began to synthesize all the information he had collected. Grouping similar data into one category, he then circled it and linked it to related categories. Gradually a huge diagram appeared, spilling onto a second sheet of paper, where the data and information were combined into conclusions.

They spent two days and two nights trying to understand and come up with a key to the enigma confronting them. Two days and two nights to conclude that—in spite of the advances of modern medicine—deep coma remains a mystery. It is a dark zone where bodies live divorced from the minds that animate them and give them souls. Exhausted, eyes reddened, Arthur fell asleep on the floor. Lauren, sitting at the drafting table, pored over the diagrams, her fingertips following the arrows. To her surprise, she noticed that the paper undulated slightly under her moving finger.

She curled up on the floor beside Arthur, rubbed her palm on the carpet, and ran her hand along his forearm. She smiled as the hairs rose, reacting to the static electricity from her hand. She stroked his head and lay there, pensive.

*W*hen Arthur awoke seven hours later, Lauren was seated at his drafting table.

He rubbed his eyes and gave her a smile she instantly returned.

"You'd have been more comfortable in your bed, but you were sleeping so soundly I didn't dare wake you."

"Have I been sleeping long?"

"Yes, but not as long as you needed to."

Arthur wanted to grab a coffee and go right back to work, but she cut him short. His commitment to helping her was very touching, but there was no point to it. He was not a doctor; she was only a resident; and unaided, they had no hope of solving the enigma of deep coma.

"Well, do you have any other ideas?"

"I think you should drink your coffee, take a nice shower, and then come for a stroll with me. You can't live shut away like a hermit in your apartment just because your houseguest is a ghost."

He agreed about the coffee, but he wished she would cut out the "ghost" stuff. She didn't look anything like a ghost. She wanted to know what he meant by that, but he refused to be drawn in. "I'll say something nice, and you'll take advantage of me."

Lauren raised her eyebrows. "What do you mean by 'nice'?" He told her just to forget it, but of course she wouldn't give in. She put her hands on her hips, planted herself in front of him, and repeated her question.

"I said forget it, Lauren. All I meant is that you're no specter."

"What am I then?"

"A woman, a very beautiful woman. Now I'm taking a shower."

He left the room without looking back. He couldn't deny it—he truly enjoyed her company. She was smart and funny and full of life. He knew he was getting in way over his head, but he let the shower pound away his doubts and emerged, half an hour later, in jeans and a heavy cashmere sweater. He announced that he felt like eating a good steak.

"It's only ten in the morning," Lauren pointed out.

"But in New York it's lunchtime, and in London it's already time for dinner."

"Yes, but we're not in New York or London."

"That won't change the way my steak tastes."

She wanted him to get back to his real life again, and told him so. He was lucky to have one—she, of all people, knew that—and he should use it. He didn't have the right to drop everything like this.

"Don't get dramatic on me, Lauren. I'm just taking a few days off."

But she insisted that he was embarking on a dangerous and ultimately pointless course.

He turned on her. "Great! It's just great to hear a doctor

talk that way. I thought that there was no such thing as a predestined outcome, that anything is possible. Why do I have greater faith than you?"

Precisely because she was a doctor, she said—because she believed she saw things clearly, because she saw that they were wasting their time, his time.

"You shouldn't get attached to me. I have nothing to offer you, nothing to share, nothing to give! I can't even make you a cup of coffee!"

"Shit. Well, if you can't make me a cup of coffee, then there's really no hope at all for the future." Arthur paused. "I'm not doing this only for you, Lauren. I'm doing it for me, too. I didn't ask to find you in my closet, but there you were. No one but me can hear you or see you or talk to you. I'm the only one who can help you, and it's the right thing to do. That's life, that's just how things are."

She was right to say that what they were doing was fraught with risk, he went on. For both of them—for her, because it might raise false hopes; for him, "because it will mess up my life. But that's just my point, that's life." He had no choice: she was there, in his apartment, "which is your apartment, too"; she was in a difficult situation and he was taking care of her: "That's what people do in a civilized world, never mind the risks involved." As he saw it, giving a dollar to a homeless man outside a supermarket was easy; it cost you nothing. "It's when you give something that you have very little of, that you truly give. Look, I know that you don't know much about me, but I'm the kind of person who decides what to do and then does it to the end, no matter what. Do believe me—the way I believed you."

He told her he had a right to try to help her. "In fact, your willingness to accept my help is about the only part of real life that you still have. You may think I'm doing this without taking the time to really think it through, and you're absolutely right. It would take me the rest of my life to think this thing through. But it's while you're thinking, while you're weighing the pros and cons, that life goes on. It passes you by while you're doing nothing. I don't know how, but we're going to get you out of this. If you were meant to die, you'd already be dead. I'm just here to give you a hand."

He concluded by asking her to accept what he was doing, if not for herself, then at least for all the people she'd be taking care of in a few years' time.

"You could have been a lawyer," Lauren said, shaking her head.

"I should have been a doctor."

"Why didn't you become one?"

"Because my mom died too early."

"How old were you?"

"Much too young," he said quietly. "Let's drop the subject."

"Why don't you want to talk about it?"

She was a physician, not a psychoanalyst, he retorted. He didn't want to talk about his mother's death because it was too painful to dwell on. He had lost his mother when he was very young, and his father even earlier. They'd given him the best of themselves, for as long as they could. "The past is the past, end of story." He paused. "So I'm not a doctor; instead I run an architectural firm. I like what I do and the people I work with." Lauren waited for him to continue. "Look, I'm still very hungry. Even if this isn't London, and I can't get a steak, I'm still going to fix myself some eggs and bacon."

She followed him into the kitchen.

"Who took care of you after your parents died?"

"You don't take no for an answer, do you?"

"Not a chance."

"This isn't the point. There are more interesting and important things to be talking about."

"I'm interested."

"Interested in what?"

"In how you happened to become capable of doing a thing like this—dropping everything to take care of the shadow of a woman you don't know. You don't even have a shot at getting in my pants; I don't have any. So I'm curious."

"Listen, I'm not hiding anything, okay? I don't need or want a shrink. I have a past that couldn't be more concrete or more complete—because it's the past, it's over."

"So I have no right to get to know you?"

"Of course you have a right. But what you're asking about right now is my past, it's not me."

"Absolutely. Your past has absolutely no influence whatsoever on who you are."

"It's private, it's not much fun to think about, and it's not the point."

"We don't have a train to catch. We've spent two days and nights studying coma—we could use a break."

"Now who should have been the lawyer!"

"Yes, but I'm a doctor. Answer me."

Without a word, Arthur rose and took his plate over to the kitchen. Lauren stayed in the living room. In a few minutes, Arthur returned to his desk.

"Have you loved many women?" she asked him softly, without looking up.

"Who counts, when you're in love?"

"Well, then, have there been many who 'counted'?"

He told her that he had fallen in love three times: once as a teenager, once as a young man, and once as a "not-so-young man"—still not quite all the way to being a full-grown man, though, "or else we'd still be together." That struck her as a fair answer, but she wanted to know why it hadn't worked out with Carol Ann. He thought it was because he was too idealistic.

"You mean possessive?" she asked.

"No, I mean idealistic. My mother filled me with stories about ideal love. Having ideals can be a heavy burden."

"Why?"

"I set my standards much too high."

"For the woman?"

"No, for myself."

She asked him to elaborate, but he refused: he didn't want to seem "old-fashioned and ridiculous." She told him to try anyway. Knowing he had no chance of deflecting her from the subject, he said, "Recognizing happiness when it's lying at your feet, having the will and the courage to reach down and take it in your arms—and to hold on to it—that's the heart's intelligence. Intelligence minus heart is just logic, and that doesn't amount to much."

"So Carol Ann left you."

Arthur did not reply.

"And you haven't quite healed."

"Oh, I've healed all right. Perhaps the problem was I was never sick."

"You couldn't love her?"

"Everyone is scared that sharing everyday life with someone means they're going to get bored and caught up in routines, but I don't believe that has to be inevitable."

"What do you believe, then?"

"I believe that everyday life with someone is the ground in which true intimacy grows. I don't think it has to create a boring rut. I believe it gives you a shot at reinventing life—the whole spectrum, from the tiny habit to the crazy gesture."

He talked about fruit left unpicked, rotting on the ground by the tree. "That's the fruit of happiness that will never be eaten, because of negligence, or habit, or holding on to stupid certitudes." Arthur believed you could grow into love. For him there was nothing more complete than time-tested love, a couple journeying together and welcoming the gradual evolution of passion into tenderness.

"Is this something you know from experience?"

"Not really. I wish!" He hesitated. "What about you? Have you ever been in love?"

"Do you know many people who haven't been in love? You want to know if I'm in love with anyone right now? No. Well, yes and no."

"Who was he?"

"He still is: thirty-eight, movie director, good-looking, unattached, a bit selfish, the ideal man . . ."

"And so?"

"It was light-years away from the sort of love you're talking about."

"Tell me about him."

She had shared four years of her life with her film director—four years of a stormy on-again, off-again drama in which the actors tore each other to pieces, then glued themselves back again time after time, as if histrionics could add another dimension to life. She said it was a selfish relationship kept alive mostly by physical passion.

"Are you very physical?"

She found the question rather funny, under the circumstances.

"You don't have to answer."

"I don't intend to. Anyway, he broke it off two months before my accident. Good for him. At least he needn't feel any sense of obligation toward me today."

"Do you miss him?"

"I missed him when we first broke up. Now I see that generosity is important in a couple."

Lauren had been through her share of relationships, all of them ending for roughly the same reasons. Some people might lose their ideals as they age, but with Lauren it was the opposite. The older she got, the more ideals she seemed to have.

"I think couples shouldn't even contemplate living together unless they're truly ready to give. Unless you have that degree of commitment, you're fooling yourself. Happiness is not just there for the taking. And I also think you're either a giver or a receiver. I give before I receive, but I've definitely had it now with selfish and complicated people, who are too stingy to make a real commitment." Sometimes, she said, it was time to take honest stock of yourself and figure out what you really wanted out of life.

Arthur thought she was taking things much too seriously.

"I've been attracted to the opposite of my ideal man for too long," she said. "Men at the other extreme from what would make me happy."

Arthur took Lauren's hand. "Come on, let's get some fresh air."

. . .

They drove in silence all the way to Ocean Beach. It had been a long morning.

When they parked, Arthur went around and opened the door for Lauren. He bowed as she got out of the car and took her hand. "I like being by the water," he said to break the silence.

Lauren did not answer at once; she was gazing at the horizon. She put her hand on Arthur's arm.

"You're not like other men."

"Is it my two noses that bother you?"

"Nothing bothers me. But you're different from the other men I've known."

"Really? In what way?"

"You're more thoughtful."

"Is that a character flaw?"

"No, but it's unusual. Nothing seems to be a problem for you."

"I don't mind problems, because I like finding solutions."

"There's more to it than that."

"Here she is again, my PPS!"

"What's a PPS?"

"My personal portable shrink."

"You don't have to answer me, but I have the right to sense things and ask about them. I'm not giving you the third degree."

"I have nothing to hide, Lauren, no dark side, no twilight zone, no secrets. I am who I am, and believe me, my shortcomings are many."

Arthur had never been crazy about himself, but he didn't

hate himself either. He was glad that he had never felt bound by conformity. Perhaps that was what she sensed. "I'm not part of any system, I've always fought that. I see the people I like, I go where I want to, I read a book because it interests me and not because everyone's talking about it. My whole life has been that way. I don't burden myself with overanalyzing everything."

The conversation resumed after they had gone inside to the welcome warmth of a nearby lounge. Arthur drank a cappuccino and munched on cookies.

"I love this place," he said, his eyes scanning the room.

On a couch, a small boy of seven or eight had curled up in his mother's arms. She was holding a book open, describing the pictures, stroking the child's cheek slowly, with tenderness. When he smiled, two dimples shone out like tiny suns. Arthur watched them for a long time.

"What are you looking at?" asked Lauren.

"That kid over there. Look at his face, he's deep in his own world."

"Does that bring back memories?"

Arthur merely smiled.

"You and your mother must have been very close."

"My mother died yesterday. It was years ago, but it feels like yesterday. The most amazing thing was, the day after she died, there were still buildings. The streets were still full of cars. People walked around. They didn't seem to realize that my whole world had just vanished. And I was empty. It was as if there were no noise in the world, as if the stars had fallen out of the sky. On the day she died—I swear it's true—the bees didn't come out of their hive in our garden. Not one of them buzzed around her roses. It was as if they knew, too. God, how I would like to be like that kid over there, just for five minutes, hidden in the curve of her arm, with her voice to soothe me to sleep. I'd like to feel that shiver down my spine when she stroked my chin to wish me good night. When I was with her nothing could bother me—not Steve Hachenbach the school bully, not Mr. Morton yelling at me for messing up my homework, not the stink in the cafeteria.

"I'll tell you why I'm 'more thoughtful,' like you said. It's because life is short, and we need to focus on the important things."

"I hope God's listening to you. My important things are still ahead of me."

"That's why it's important that we not give up." He rose. "C'mon, let's go home and get back to work."

Arthur paid the check and they walked to the parking lot. Before he got back in the car, Lauren kissed him on the cheek. "Thanks for everything," she said. Arthur smiled, blushed, and wordlessly opened the door.

Chapter
EIGHT

*A*rthur spent most of the next three weeks in the San Francisco Public Library, an imposing turn-of-the-century building in the neoclassical style. There were dozens of rooms with lofty vaulted ceilings, and an atmosphere that was unusual for a library. Nob Hill aristocrats crossed paths with ancient hippies they'd grown up with, exchanging anecdotes and points of view on city history. The medical books were kept in Room 27. Arthur sat in Row 48, the one closest to the neurology section. There he scanned thousands of pages on coma, unconsciousness, and cranial trauma.

Although the texts gave him a clearer understanding of Lauren's problem, they brought him no closer to figuring out how to help her get back into her body. After his reading, he spent evenings e-mailing eminent professors of medicine and researchers describing his dilemma, pretending he was working on a novel. Some of them answered. They all agreed—the situation he described was medically impossible.

Every evening Arthur returned to find Lauren waiting for him. He'd make dinner and tell her about the day's research, trying to put the most positive spin on it he could. They'd embark on long discussions; Lauren often forgot that Arthur had never studied medicine. He had acquired an expert medical vocabulary with amazing speed, and they often talked until late into the night. In the morning, over breakfast, he would describe what he planned to research that day. He refused to let her come along, saying her presence would distract him. But though Arthur maintained a resolute optimism—he never let himself seem discouraged in front of Lauren—every silence echoed. They were getting nowhere.

On the Thursday of his third week of research, he left the library early. He turned Marvin Gaye up loud on the car stereo. A smiled creased his lips, and he abruptly turned onto California Street to buy some food. He hadn't made any breakthroughs, but he suddenly felt like a celebration dinner. He'd make the table look nice, light some candles, flood the apartment with music. He would ask Lauren to dance, and he would forbid any discussion of medicine.

*A*rthur drove up to the building on Green Street just as the bay faded into its magical twilight.

He skipped up the stairs, performed a balancing act to get the key in the lock, and went inside, arms loaded with packages. He pushed the door shut with his foot and set the bags down on the kitchen counter.

Lauren was sitting on the window seat in the living room, watching the view. She didn't even turn around.

"Hey, what's wrong?" Arthur asked. As he walked over, she suddenly disappeared. He could hear her now in the bedroom, wailing, "And I can't even slam a door!"

"Did something happen?" he called after her.

"Leave me alone!"

Arthur took off his coat and went into the bedroom. When he opened the door, he saw Lauren leaning against the window, her head in her hands.

"Are you crying?"

"I can't cry."

"You're sobbing! What's going on?"

"Nothing."

He wanted to look her in the eye, but she turned her back. "Leave me alone." Arthur placed his hands on her shoulders and turned her around to face him. He raised her lowered head with the tip of his finger. "Tell me what's wrong."

"They're going to end it."

"Who's going to end what?"

"I went to the hospital this morning. Mom was there, talking to me. She's been having meetings with the ethical committee. They've decided it's time to remove my feeding tube."

"What does that mean?"

"It means I'm going to die."

*T*he hospital's ethics committee had contacted Lauren's mother that morning. She had gone to Memorial Hospital and found three of its members waiting for her in Lauren's room. An older woman, Dr. Colonna, had led her by the arm into another room, invited her to sit, and then led the discussion. There had been a long lecture. Dr. Colonna had employed all kinds of arguments to persuade Mrs. Kline to come to terms with the inevitable. Lauren was no longer a mind or a spirit, only a body, and one that was being kept alive at an exorbitant cost to society. It was easier on the family to keep a loved one artificially alive than to decide to accept death, but at what price? Mrs. Kline had to accept the unacceptable. There was no need to feel guilty. They had tried everything; the case was hopeless. They all had to have the courage to admit it. Dr. Colonna emphasized that Mrs. Kline was becoming emotionally dependent on her daughter's body.

Mrs. Kline had pulled away, shaking her head in horror. She could not, would not, authorize them to stop feeding Lauren. But the doctor's practiced logic progressively chiseled away at Mrs. Kline's resistance to the decision that she was hearing described so persuasively as "rational and humane." Refusal, Dr. Colonna intimated, would be unjust, cruel—both for the patient and her mother. It would be selfish, even unhealthy.

Doubt began gaining ground. The counselor kept working her arguments, subtly alternating guilt with sympathy. The bed that Lauren occupied could be given to another patient, one with hope of survival. One kind of guilt was substituted for another. After several hours, Mrs. Kline cracked. In tears, she replied that she would think about euthanizing Lauren. Her only condition was that they wait four days, "to be sure." It was Thursday. She needed to know that nothing would be done before Monday. She needed to prepare herself. Compassionately, the doctor bowed her head, miming sympathy and understanding, masking her deep satisfaction that this mother had resolved a situation that could not be solved by science: what to do with a human being who was neither dead nor alive. Hippocrates had never considered the possibility that medical science might one day confront this kind of drama.

The doctors departed, leaving Mrs. Kline alone to be with her daughter. She took Lauren's hand, placed her head on Lauren's stomach, and, in tears, she asked her forgiveness. "I can't do this anymore, my love, my little girl," she said. "I wish it were me in your place." At the other end of the room, Lauren watched her—filled with a mixture of fear, sadness, and horror. She had come up behind her mother to hug her shoulders, but Mrs. Kline felt nothing. Lauren tried with every fiber of whatever she was now to give her mother a sign, to move merely a finger, a toe—to no avail. Finally, Lauren left her mother, left her own body. She had wandered about, like a ghost.

$\mathcal{B}$y the elevator, Dr. Colonna and her colleagues were congratulating themselves.

"Aren't you worried she'll change her mind?" Fernstein asked.

"I don't think she will," Dr. Colonna answered. "And we could always talk it through again."

$\mathcal{L}$auren bowed her head now and moved back to the windowsill, determined to soak in the light, the view, the smells, and the movement of the city. "Today's Thursday," she said. "I have only a few more days to live."

Arthur took her in his arms, enveloping her in tenderness. "You're so beautiful, even when you're crying. Dry your eyes. I won't let them do it."

"How will you stop them?"

"Give me a couple of hours to think about it."

She moved out of his arms and turned back to the window. "What's the point?" she said, staring at the streetlamp below. "Maybe it's for the best; maybe they're right."

"What do you mean, 'it's for the best'?" His tone of voice was aggressive; she didn't answer. Lauren was such a determined person most of the time, but now she seemed to have resigned herself. "The truth is, all I have left is a shadow of real life. I'll never come back. Besides, I'm ruining my mother's life."

"Do you really think your mother would be relieved if you died for good?"

Lauren couldn't help but smile. "Thanks for that."

"What did I say?"

"It's just the expression 'died for good.' Under the circumstances, you know."

"Do you believe your mom could ever fill the empty space you'd leave behind? Do you truly think it's best for her if you give up? And what about me?"

She looked at him inquiringly. "What about you?"

"I'll be there when you wake up. You may be invisible to other people, but not to me."

"Is that a declaration?"

Now she was mocking him. "Don't be so full of yourself," he said dryly.

"Why are you doing all this for me?" she said, almost angrily. "Hanging around me, making plans, fighting on my behalf? What's wrong with you?" Now she was practically yelling at him. "What's your motive?"

"Don't be nasty, Lauren."

"Answer me, answer honestly!"

"Sit here beside me and calm down. I'm going to tell you a story. It's a real story, and then you'll understand it. It happened one day when I was about seven, at a dinner at our house near Carmel."

Arthur told her a story that an old friend of his parents', a famous eye surgeon, had told that evening around the dinner table. Dr. Miller had seemed oddly preoccupied, and Arthur's mother had asked him what was wrong. He explained that two weeks previously, he had operated on a little girl who'd been blind since birth. She didn't know what she looked like, had no concept of the sky, could not imagine colors, had never even seen her mother's face. The outside world was unknown to her; no external image had ever entered her brain. She had guessed at shapes all her life, but she had never been able to associate a mental image with the contours that she felt with her hands.

And so Coco, which is what everyone called Dr. Miller, had decided to perform an intricate and risky operation, an "impossible" operation. The morning before Arthur's parents' dinner, alone in the hospital room with that little girl, he had taken off the bandages.

"You'll start to see things before I'm through taking off these dressings," he told her. "Are you ready?"

"What am I going to see?" she asked.

"I've already told you, you'll see light."

"What *is* light?"

"It's life . . . just a minute . . ."

And a few seconds later, just as he had promised, the light of day entered her eyes. It raced across her pupils, faster than a river freed of a dam, sped across the vitreous matter and transported to the back of the eyes the billions of pieces of information it contained. Stimulated for the first time since the birth of the child, the millions of cells in her retinas triggered a wonderfully complex chemical reaction to codify the images imprinted upon them. The codes were instantly transmitted to the two optic nerves, just roused from dormancy and yet nonetheless able to pass this enormous volume of information to the brain. In a few thousandths of a second, the brain decoded the data it had received, leaving it to the consciousness to associate and make sense of it all. The most ancient of image processors, the most complex and the smallest in the world, had suddenly been linked to an optical system and was now at work.

Impatient, but frightened, the little girl took Coco's hand and said, "Wait, I'm scared." He stopped removing the dressings, took her in his arms, and told her all over again what would happen when he was through. There would be hundreds of new items of information to absorb, understand, and compare with everything her imagination had constructed. Then Coco resumed his removal of the bandages.

When she opened her eyes, she looked first at her hands; she moved them up and down and sideways, like puppets. She tipped her head to one side, smiled, laughed—wept, too—still not tearing her eyes away from her ten fingers. Maybe it was to escape looking at everything else that was becoming real around her, because she was certainly terrified. Then she directed her gaze at her rag doll, which had kept her company through her dark nights and days.

The door opened at the far end of the big room, and her mother came in. She didn't say a word. The little girl raised her head and looked. She had never seen her mother before. And yet, even though her mother was still yards away, the child's face changed and she opened her arms wide, and without a moment's hesitation she called this "stranger" Mommy.

"When Coco finished telling his story, I realized that for the rest of his life he would possess a tremendous strength: he had done something important. So just tell yourself that what I'm doing now, for you, is in memory of Coco Miller. And now, if you've calmed down, you need to leave me to think."

Lauren was silent. Arthur settled onto the sofa and started gnawing at a pencil. He remained like that for several minutes, then leaped up, sat down at his desk, and commenced scribbling on a piece of paper. He took about an hour, while Lauren watched him, looking like a cat gazing, puzzled, at an insect. Her head was slightly tilted, and every time Arthur started to write, or suddenly stopped and gnawed some more, she looked askance. When he finished, he turned to her, his expression serious.

"What kind of treatments are they giving you, at the hospital?"

"You mean aside from hygiene?"

"I mean the medical care."

Lauren described being fed intravenously, since she could neither eat nor drink. Three times a week, antibiotics were injected into the drip feed as a precautionary measure. Her hips, elbows, knees, and shoulders were massaged to prevent bedsores. Most of the rest was just checking her temperature and heartbeat and so on. She didn't need a breathing tube.

"My heart and lungs can function, so I'm breathing on my own. That's their whole problem. Otherwise they could simply pull the plug."

"So why do they say it all costs so much?"

"Because of the bed."

Lauren explained that in most hospitals there was no real distinction between the kinds of care given to different types of patient. You just divided the cost of running a hospital by the number of beds occupied in a year. Inevitably, it came to a fortune.

"Maybe we can solve our problem and theirs in one swoop," Arthur said.

"What have you come up with?"

"Have you ever looked after a patient in deep coma?"

She had, for people brought in after an emergency, but only for short periods, never long stays. "But if you had to?" Arthur pressed her. She supposed it wouldn't be a problem, it was almost more a nurse's kind of work, unless there was a sudden complication.

"So you would know how to do it?" Arthur continued, urgently. She couldn't see what he was getting at. "Is the IV very complex?" he insisted.

"In what way?"

"To get one. Can you find them in pharmacies?"

"In the hospital pharmacy, sure."

"But in a normal pharmacy?"

She thought for a few seconds, then nodded. The drip feed could be reconstituted by buying glucose, anticoagulants, saline, and so forth and blending them together. It was feasible. Besides, people on home care had their IV fluids and food administered by nurses, who ordered the products from a pharmacy.

"I have to bring Paul into this," Arthur said.

"What for?"

"For the ambulance."

"The ambulance? What are you planning?"

"We're going to kidnap you."

"What?" Now she was getting worried.

"We're going to kidnap you. No body, no euthanasia!"

"You're out of your mind!"

"Not completely."

"How can we kidnap me? Where will we hide the body? Who'll take care of it?"

"One question at a time!"

She would take care of her body, or else she'd teach him how to; she had the necessary experience. They just had to obtain the fluids necessary for the IV, but according to her that should not be too difficult. They might just have to change pharmacies every so often, or something, to avoid detection.

"Who will write the prescriptions?" she asked.

"That takes us back to your first question: How?"

"And?"

"Paul's stepfather runs an auto-body shop; they specialize in rescue vehicles brought in by firefighters, police, emergency services. We can 'borrow' an ambulance. It can't be that hard. We'll get our hands on a pair of white scrub suits and take you out of the hospital."

Lauren gave a nervous laugh. "Wait a minute. It's not that simple!"

She reminded him that entering a hospital was not like going to the supermarket. Getting out of one was even more complicated. Transferring a patient involved a number of administrative steps. You needed a certificate of admission from the hospital that was planning to care for the patient. There had to be an authorization for the patient's transfer signed by the doctor in charge of the case, a requisition from the ambulance company, and a statement regarding the patient's condition and the requirements during transport.

"That's where you come in, Lauren, you're going to help me get all that paperwork."

"But how can I—I can't even carry anything."

"But you know where the forms are kept."

"Yes. So?"

"So I'm the one who'll steal them. Are you familiar with what they look like?"

"Of course. I often arranged transfers." She went on to describe them: just typical forms, printed on white, pink, and blue paper, with the letterhead of the hospital or ambulance service.

"We'll get our hands on some and forge them," he said excitedly. "Come on, let's go."

Arthur grabbed his jacket and keys and ordered Lauren to follow him, in a tone that allowed her no leeway to oppose his far-fetched plan. They got in the car and drove out onto Green Street. He drove fast to Memorial Hospital and headed straight for the emergency-services parking lot. When Lauren asked what he was going to do, he replied with a faint smile at the corners of his mouth, "Follow me and keep a straight face!"

As he was going through the first door of the emergency bay, Arthur bent over double and groped his way to the reception desk. The nurse on duty asked him what was wrong. He described violent cramps that had set in two hours after dinner, and made it clear he'd already had his appendix removed. The nurse told him to lie down in an examining room and wait for a doctor to attend to him. Perched on the arm of a wheelchair, Lauren was beginning to smile broadly. Arthur was playing his part perfectly. Even she had been worried when he had first collapsed on entering the waiting room.

"You don't know what you're getting yourself into," she murmured as a doctor came in to examine him.

*D*r. Spacek introduced himself and drew the curtain around the cubicle. He had Arthur lie down on the examination table and asked about his symptoms while scanning Arthur's file. There had been so many questions, it seemed the file contained his entire medical and personal history. Arthur said he was suffering from terrible cramps.

"Can you point to where it hurts the most?" asked the doctor.

"No, it's everywhere, all over my stomach; I feel as sick as a dog."

"Don't lay it on so thick," whispered Lauren. "He'll give you a shot of tranquilizers, have you spend the night here, and tomorrow morning you'll get a barium enema, a fibroscopy, and a colonoscopy."

"No shots!" Arthur blurted out.

"I didn't say anything about shots," observed Dr. Spacek, looking up from his folder.

"No, but I'd just as soon say so right away because I hate shots."

The doctor asked him whether he was nervous by nature, and Arthur nodded.

"Now I'm going to palpate your abdomen to find out

where the pain is sharpest." Arthur nodded again. The doctor placed his hands one on top of the other and began to press on every inch of Arthur's abdomen.

"Does it hurt here?"

"Uh, yes," he said hesitantly.

"Here?"

"No, you're not supposed to hurt there," whispered Lauren with a smile, and Arthur at once denied any discomfort.

Lauren continued to guide Arthur throughout the examination. The doctor diagnosed colon spasms due to stress and handed Arthur a prescription for an antispasmodic medication. Two handshakes and three "Thank you, Doctor"s later, Arthur was striding down the long corridor that led to the exit. In his hand he had three different forms, all with Memorial Hospital's letterhead and logo. One blue, one pink, one green. One was a prescription, one was a receipt itemizing services and charges, and the third was a form headed, in large capitals, AUTHORIZATION FOR TRANS-FER/AUTHORIZATION FOR DISCHARGE, and below, in italic type, *Circle one*. He was grinning broadly, proud of himself. Lauren walked beside him. He put his arm around her. "We make a pretty good team, don't we?"

Back at the apartment, he slipped the three documents into his computer scanner and copied them. Now he possessed an unlimited source of printed forms of every shape and color with the hospital's official letterhead.

"You're very good," said Lauren as the first official-looking forms emerged from the color printer.

"I'll call Paul."

"Not until we've talked about your plan a little, please."

"You're right. I need to quiz you more about this whole procedure of transferring a patient."

But that was not what she wanted to discuss. "Arthur, I'm very touched, but let's face it, your plan is unrealistic, it's crazy, and it's much too dangerous for you. You'll go to jail if you're caught. And for what?"

"Isn't it a lot riskier for you if we don't try to do something? We only have four days, Lauren!"

"You can't do it, Arthur, I don't have the right to let you go ahead. Sorry."

"I once knew a girl who said sorry whenever she opened her mouth. It got to the point where her friends were too scared to offer her a glass of water, for fear she'd apologize for being thirsty."

"Arthur, don't kid around. It's a crazy plan."

"It's the situation that's crazy, Lauren. I don't have any other option."

"I won't let you take these kinds of risks for me."

"Lauren, you've got to help. We're wasting time. It's your life that's at stake."

"There has to be some other way."

Arthur could see only one alternative to his plan. He could try to talk to Lauren's mother and dissuade her from authorizing the hospital to remove Lauren's drip. But it would be difficult. They had never met, and she wasn't likely to agree to meet a total stranger. He could pretend to be an old friend of Lauren's, but she'd be suspicious—she must know all Lauren's close friends. Perhaps he could run into her by accident? Somewhere she went often? They'd have to think of a place.

Lauren was silent for a moment. "She walks the dog in the Marina Green every morning," she said.

"Yes, but then I'd have to have a dog to walk, too."

"Why?"

"Because if I take a leash for a walk with no dog on the other end, my credibility will be shot."

"Ha, ha, ha. Then just go jogging."

She liked the idea. He could time his run to coincide with Kali's walk. He'd come over to pat the dog, make a fuss over her, and after that it would be easy to strike up a conversation with Lauren's mother. Arthur said he'd try it.

Early the next morning he put on sweatpants and a sweatshirt. Before leaving, he asked Lauren to hold him tight in her arms.

"What's with you today?" she asked shyly.

"Nothing. I don't have time to explain. It's for the dog."

She laid her head on his shoulder, sighing. "That's fine," he said briskly, and pulled away. "Now I'm off, otherwise I'll miss her." Without even taking the time to say good-bye, he rushed out of the apartment. The door closed. Lauren shrugged and said to herself, "He hugs me because of the dog."

The Golden Gate was still sleeping under a blanket of fog when Arthur arrived. Only the pinnacles of the red bridge emerged from the mist. The sea was calm in the prison of the bay, the early-morning gulls making wide, circular sweeps in their quest for fish. The sprawling lawns bordering the bay were still soaked in the night's sea spray, and the moored boats bobbed gently on the water. Everything was peaceful; a few early joggers cut through the foggy air. In a few hours, a fat sun would crest the heights of Sausalito and Tiburon and free the red bridge from its shroud.

Arthur spotted Lauren's mother from a long way off, matching perfectly the description her daughter had given him. Kali trotted a few steps ahead of her. Mrs. Kline seemed lost in thought, heavy with pain. As she approached Arthur, Kali suddenly stopped short, sniffing the air with a circling movement of her muzzle and head. She came closer, sniffing the bottom of Arthur's leg, and then she lay down at his feet, whimpering, her tail thumping the ground. Kali was trembling with joy and excitement. Arthur knelt down and began to stroke her gently. The dog licked his hand, her plaintive whines growing louder and more urgent.

Lauren's mother drew near, looking greatly surprised. "Do you know each other?"

"Why do you ask?" Arthur said as he rose.

"She's usually so fearful, nobody can get close to her. But she's falling all over you."

"Well, I don't know. Maybe. She does look awfully like the dog of a friend I used to like a lot."

"Yes?" said Mrs. Kline, her heart beginning to race.

The dog sat up and began to yap, holding out her paw to Arthur. "Kali!" exclaimed Lauren's mother. "Leave the gentleman alone." Arthur stuck out his hand and introduced himself. After a moment's hesitation Mrs. Kline took his hand but did not introduce herself. She was disturbed by her dog's behavior, and she apologized to Arthur for Kali's excess of familiarity.

"No problem. Dogs like me. I think they can tell I like them. She's really cute. It's unbelievable how much she looks like Lauren's dog."

Mrs. Kline suddenly looked dizzy. Her face tensed.

"Are you all right, ma'am?" asked Arthur, taking her hand.

"You knew my daughter?"

"So this *is* Lauren's dog—you're her mother?"

"You knew her?"

"Well, yes—we were quite close."

She told him she had never heard Lauren mention him and asked how they had met. He told her he was an architect. He had met Lauren at the hospital when she stitched up his hand after an accident with a box cutter. They had hit it off and saw each other fairly often. "Every now and then I dropped by and had lunch with her at the hospital, and we sometimes met for dinner when she finished early."

"Lauren never had time for lunch, and she always got home late," her mother said suspiciously.

Arthur lowered his head and said nothing.

"But Kali does seem to know you."

"I'm more sorry than I can say about what happened to Lauren, ma'am. I've visited her at the hospital several times."

"I've never seen you there."

He asked if he could stroll with her a little. They walked by the water. Arthur ventured to ask for news about Lauren's condition, explaining that he had not been able to see her for some time. Mrs. Kline told him the situation had not improved, that there was no longer any hope. She said nothing of the decision she had reached, but she described her daughter's condition in resolutely bleak terms.

After a few moments' silence, Arthur began to plead for continued hope. "Doctors don't know everything about coma" . . . "Coma patients can hear us" . . . "Some patients have come back after years" . . . "Life is sacred, and when it keeps going it's a sign" . . . He even invoked God, as "the only one with the right to dispense life and death."

Mrs. Kline suddenly stopped walking and looked Arthur straight in the eyes. "You didn't just run into me now by accident, did you? Who are you and what do you want?"

"I was just out running, ma'am, and if you believe this wasn't just a chance meeting, you have to ask yourself why. I didn't teach Lauren's dog to come to me without being called."

"What do you want from me? And what right do you have to preach to me about life and death? You don't know how it feels to be there every day, to see her lying there, inert, unresponsive, not moving even an eyelash, to see her chest rising and falling but her face closed to the world."

In a burst of anger, she told him about the days and nights she had spent talking to Lauren in the vain hope that Lauren might hear. Her life had ended with her daughter's accident, leaving her an empty existence spent waiting for a call from the hospital to say it was all over. She had given her daughter life. Every day of her childhood she had woken her, dressed her, and taken her to school; every evening she had tucked her in and told her a story. She had listened to her joys and torments. "When she was a teenager, I accepted her anger, shared her first loves, worked with her on her studies. I faded into the background when I needed to, and even when she was alive I missed her, after she left home. Every day of my life, my first thought in the morning has been for her, and the last one at night. . . ."

Mrs. Kline broke off and began to weep. Arthur put his hand on her shoulder and said he was sorry.

"I can't go on," she muttered. "I'm sorry. Please leave me; I should never have spoken to you."

Arthur apologized again, patted the dog's head, and

walked slowly away. He got into his car, and as he drove away, he saw Lauren's mother in the rearview mirror, watching him leave.

When he reached his apartment, Lauren was balancing on the edge of the coffee table.

"What are you doing?" he asked.

"Practicing."

"I see."

"How did it go?"

He gave her a detailed account of the meeting and said how disappointed he was at his failure to sway her mother.

"You never had much of a chance, really. She never changes her mind, especially if it's a decision she's taken a long, hard time to reach. She's stubborn as a mule."

"Don't be hard on her, she's going through hell."

"What a son-in-law you would make!"

"What exactly do you mean by that?"

"Nothing. You're just the kind of guy mothers adore."

"That's a bit beside the point, isn't it?"

"True. You'd be a widower before you could marry me."

"Is that a proposal?"

"No. Forget I spoke." Lauren looked depressed. "This has been a really bad morning. I need to be alone." With that, she disappeared, leaving Arthur alone and perplexed in the apartment. He sat down at his desk, turned on the computer, and started typing. He'd made his decision in the car, driving home from the Marina. There was no alternative, and they would have to act quickly. On Monday, the doctors would remove Lauren's feeding tube, and she would die. He typed out a list of items they would need for his plan, printed out the file, and picked up the phone to call Paul.

"I have to see you as soon as possible."

"Aha, you're back from the wilds!"

"It's urgent, Paul. I need you."

"Where do you want to meet?"

"Wherever you like."

"Come to my place."

Half an hour later Paul let him in. They sat on couches in the living room.

"What's up?"

"I need you to do me a favor with no questions asked. I want you to help me kidnap a body from the hospital."

"What is this, a horror movie? You're through with the ghost, and now you want a corpse? I can give you mine if you keep this up—it'll be available."

"It isn't a corpse."

"What is it, then? A hospital patient in the peak of health?"

"I'm serious, Paul, and we're in a hurry."

"I'm not allowed to ask questions?"

"You'd have a hard time understanding the answers."

"Because I'm too dumb?"

"Because no one could believe what I'm going through."

"Try me."

"I want you to help me remove the body of a woman in a coma. They're going to terminate her on Monday. And I'm not going to let them."

"You've fallen in love with a woman in a coma? Is that what that ghost business was all about?"

Arthur mumbled a vague "Uh-huh."

Paul, who had been leaning forward alertly, fell back on the couch and sighed deeply. "This is going to cost you a couple of thousand hours with a shrink. Listen, I've gone along with you for weeks, Arthur. But I'm your friend and I have a responsibility to stop you from doing something crazy. Have you really thought this through? Your mind's made up?"

"With or without you, I'm going to do it."

"You really love to keep things simple, don't you?"

"If you don't want to get involved, just say so."

"Let's see if I have it straight. You show up looking like hell and ask me to risk ten years in jail to help you lift a body from a hospital. I think I'll just pray to be transformed into the Dalai Lama, it's my only chance. So, what exactly do you need from me?"

Arthur explained his plan and what he needed from Paul: basically, an ambulance. They could borrow one from Paul's stepfather's body shop.

"Oh, it gets even better! Now I get to rob my mother's husband! It's good to know you, pal, my life would never have been the same without you."

"I know I'm asking a lot. But I swear on my mother's grave, Paul, I have to do this. I have to do this more than I've ever had to do anything in my life."

That got Paul's attention. He knew Arthur would never invoke his mother's name except in matters of life and death. "Okay, when do you need it?"

Arthur wanted to use the ambulance on Sunday night. The best time to steal the body was at eleven PM, when the staff was changing shifts. Paul should pick him up in the ambulance at half past ten. Arthur would call him again early tomorrow morning to fine-tune the details. Arthur hugged his friend hard. Looking preoccupied, Paul walked Arthur to his car.

"Thank you," said Arthur through the window.

"That's what friends are for. Next month I may ask you to help me climb a mountain to give a manicure to a grizzly bear. Go on, get out of here, you look as though you've lots more to do."

As the car crossed the intersection and disappeared, Paul raised his arms heavenward and shouted, "Why me?" He waited for several moments, and when it seemed clear that no answer was forthcoming, he shrugged and muttered, "Yeah, I know, I know. Why not?"

*T*he next day, Arthur raced from pharmacy to pharmacy, loading his car's trunk with medical supplies. Back in the apartment, he found Lauren resting on his bed. He sat down carefully beside her and passed his hand just above her hair, not touching it. Then he whispered, "You know, you're really very beautiful." He left just as quietly as he had entered and went back to his drafting table in the living room. As soon as he was out of the room, Lauren opened her eyes and smiled.

In the living room, Arthur picked up the administrative forms he had printed the day before and began filling them in, leaving an occasional blank. Then he put everything in a folder. He took the folder, put on his jacket, went down to the car, and drove to the hospital. He parked in the lot by the emergency entrance and moved stealthily through the automatic doors. He turned and headed for the staff lounge. A nurse taking a break there addressed him. "Excuse me, can I help you?"

He explained that he was springing a surprise on an old friend who worked there. "Perhaps you know her; her name is Lauren Kline."

The nurse fell silent, and it took her a moment to find her words. "When did you see her last?"

"Oh, last summer." On the spur of the moment he improvised that he was a photojournalist just back from Africa, and Lauren was his cousin by marriage. "We're very close. Doesn't she work here anymore?"

The nurse avoided the question and told him to ask at the information desk next to admissions in the main hospital. She was sorry, but Lauren was not here in this department. Arthur put on an anxious face and asked whether there was some kind of problem. Clearly ill at ease, the nurse again told him the information desk should be able to help him. Not the ER reception desk, she added, but the one in the main hospital.

"Do I have to leave the building to get there?"

"In theory, yes. You're supposed to go back out and around."

Instead, she told him, he could take a shortcut through the building to the hospital lobby. Carefully maintaining his anxious expression, he thanked her and said good-bye. Once out of the nurse's sight, he slipped from corridor to corridor until he found what he was looking for. Through a half-open door he spied two white coats on hangers. He went in, snatched them down, and bundled them under his coat. In the pocket of one he felt a stethoscope. Then he was out in the corridor again, following the nurse's directions until he emerged from the main hospital entrance. He walked around the building, found his car in the ER parking lot, and went home.

Lauren was seated at his desk, reading the details of his plan. Before he was across the threshold, she exclaimed,

"You're out of your mind!" Without replying, he showed her the two white coats.

"I suppose you have an ambulance in the garage?"

"Paul's in charge of the ambulance. He'll have it when he picks me up at ten-thirty tomorrow night."

"Where did you get the coats?"

"At your hospital."

"Is there anything that can stop you once you've made up your mind to do something? Show me the name tags."

Arthur put on one of the lab coats, took a few steps, and turned, like a fashion model on a runway.

"What do you think?"

"You've stolen Brunswick's coat!"

"Who's he?"

"A big-name cardiologist. There's going to be hell to pay at the hospital when he notices it's missing. I can just imagine the flurry of memos. Security's going to get an earful. Brunswick is the most arrogant and foul-tempered medic in the whole hospital."

"What are the chances of someone realizing I'm not Brunswick?"

She told him not to worry. The risk was small; it would take really bad luck. Brunswick was normally around in the daytime on weekdays. The night-shift staff and the weekend personnel probably didn't know him by sight. Arthur wasn't likely to encounter a member of Brunswick's team. On Sunday night, it would be a different hospital, with different people and a different atmosphere.

"And look, I even have a stethoscope!"

"Hang it around your neck."

He did so.

"You know what? You make a terribly sexy doctor," she said, her voice soft and very feminine.

Arthur looked down at his feet. She took his hand and stroked his fingers and said in the same sweet voice, "Thank you for all you're doing for me. No one has ever taken care of me like this."

"Superman to the rescue, Lois," he said, pulling away.

They looked into each other's eyes. He took her in his arms, placed his hand on the back of her neck, and brought her head to rest on his shoulder. "We have a lot to do," he told her. "I have to get back to work."

He returned to his desk. Lauren looked at him intently and then silently withdrew to the bedroom, leaving the door open. He worked late into the night, stopping only for a light snack. He concentrated on his notes as he typed out line after line of text on his screen. He heard the television go on. "How did you do that?" he called out. She did not reply. He stood up, crossed the living room, and peeked through the doorway. Lauren was on the bed, lying flat on her stomach. She turned away from the TV screen and gave him a coy smile. He smiled back and returned to his keyboard. Once he was sure that she was absorbed in her program, he got up and went to his writing desk. He opened a drawer and pulled out a sealed letter and a key ring with old keys, big and heavy. He did not read the letter, but slipped the envelope into his coat pocket along with the keys. He returned to his computer and made a printout of his plan of action.

He headed for the bedroom, where Lauren was sitting on the foot of the bed watching Larry King. Her hair fell loose over her shoulders, and she seemed calm, peaceful.

"Everything's as ready as it will ever be," he said.

He went into the bathroom. As she heard him shower-
ing, she idly passed her hand again over the carpet. As she
stroked it, she could feel the carpet fibers lifting up with the
static electricity. He came out, wrapped in a bathrobe.

"I'll go to bed now. I have to be in shape tomorrow."

She went up to him and softly kissed his forehead. "Good
night," she said. "See you tomorrow." She left the room.

*T*he next day went by with the lazy rhythm typical of Sun-
days. The sun played hide-and-seek with drizzling clouds.
From time to time, Lauren would look up and stare hard at
Arthur, asking him if he was sure that he wanted to go
through with the plan. He no longer answered this question. In the middle of the day they went for a walk by the
ocean.

Arthur placed his arm around her shoulders. "Let's walk
over by the water. I want to tell you something."

They walked up the beach. "Take a look at all this: the
angry ocean, the trees, the changing color and intensity of
the light, the birds swooping overhead, the fish looking for
other fish to eat while hoping they won't end up as seagull
food themselves. The sounds, the waves, the wind, and the
sand, all in harmony. And right in the middle of this unbelievable symphony of life and energy, there's you and me
and every other human being on earth. But how many of us
ever really see these things? How many realize what a privi-
lege it is to wake up in the morning and see, feel, touch,
hear? Not many people are capable of forgetting their worries for the second it takes to marvel at the world around
them. People pay so little attention to their own lives. You're
aware of yours because you're in danger, and that makes

you unique. So, to answer the question you keep asking me: unless I take a few risks, all this beauty, all this energy, will become inaccessible to you forever. That's why I'm doing this, because fighting to bring you back into the world gives my life meaning. How often will I have the chance to do something so important?"

Lauren didn't say a word. After a moment, she lowered her eyes and stared at the sand. They walked side by side back to the car.

Chapter
NINE

*A*t ten-thirty on the dot Paul pulled up to Arthur's driveway, leaving the ambulance idling as he walked up the outside stairs and rang the bell. "All set," he announced when Arthur opened the door.

Arthur handed him a bag. "Put this coat on, and wear these glasses. They're just plain lenses."

"No false beards?"

Arthur ignored the joke. "I'll explain everything on the way," he said impatiently. "We've got to hurry. We have to do this during the shift change at eleven. Lauren, you come with us, we're going to need you."

"Talking to your ghost?" said Paul.

"To someone who's with us, even though you can't see her."

"Is this all some kind of joke, Arthur, or have you gone insane?"

"It's neither. It's incomprehensible, so I won't bother explaining. Come on, get moving!"

Lauren sat waiting for them in the front seat.

"Boy, this thing is old," Arthur said as he got in between Paul and Lauren. "What is this, prewar?"

"Well, excuse me," Paul said, annoyed. "I took what I could find, and now you're going to give me a hard time!"

"No, I'm sorry. It's perfect."

"Want the flashing lights and siren, Doc?"

"Paul, this is a matter of life and death. Please be serious."

"Can't do it, old pal. Absolutely not. If I seriously believed that my business partner and I were in a stolen ambulance on the way to stealing a body from a hospital, I might wake up, and your little plan would be dead in the water. So I'm doing my best to be as unserious as possible. That way I'll go on thinking this is just a dream, verging on a nightmare. On the bright side, I've always found Sunday evenings very dull; at least this will be memorable."

Lauren laughed.

"You find that funny?"

"Stop talking to yourself!"

"I'm not talking to myself."

"Okay, there's a ghost in the back! But stop having conversations with it. It makes me nervous."

"Not *it*. Her! She's a woman, and she can hear everything you say."

"I don't know what you've been smoking for the past few weeks, but I'd really like some too."

"Drive!"

"Are you two always like this?" asked Lauren.

"Pretty much."

"What did you say?" asked Paul.

"I wasn't talking to you."

Paul braked abruptly.

"What's the matter?" asked Arthur.

"Stop this! You're going too far, I swear!"

"What am I doing?"

"You know perfectly well," Paul bellowed. "You keep talking to yourself. It's absurd!"

"I'm not talking to myself, Paul, I'm talking to Lauren. You just have to take my word for it."

"Arthur, maybe this all has to stop right here and now. This is complete madness!"

Arthur raised his voice. "For God's sake, I'm asking you to trust me!"

"I want you to explain this to me!" Paul yelled. "Right now you're acting like a lunatic. You're embarking on an insane adventure, you're talking to yourself, you believe in some stupid ghost story, and you're getting me involved in it, too!"

"Just drive, Paul! I'll try to explain, but you have to do your bit and try to understand."

So as the ambulance wound its way across the city, Arthur explained the unexplainable to his lifelong friend and accomplice. He told him everything—from the beginning, from the bathroom closet to that very night.

Forgetting for a moment that Lauren was there, Arthur added, "She's beautiful, Paul, and she's funny, and witty, and we talk about everything. Sure, we disagree and bicker sometimes, but an amazing tenderness has grown between us. I feel at home with her."

Paul cut in, "If she's really here, you've landed yourself in deep trouble, my friend."

"How so?" Arthur asked, looking at Paul.

"Because," said Paul with a complacent smile, "I think you just told her you're in love." Paul glanced over at his friend, then added, "In any case, you believe your story."

"Of course I believe it. But why do you say that?"

"Because I swear you just blushed, and I've never seen you blush before." Then Paul called out, "Are you there, young lady whose body we're going to steal? If you are, you can take it from me that my buddy here has it bad. I've never seen him like this before."

Deliberately avoiding eye contact with Lauren, Arthur interjected, "Shut up and drive."

"I'll tell you what. I'm going to believe your story, Arthur. You're my friend, so I don't have any choice. Being a friend is all about being willing to act as crazy as the other guy, right? Hey, there's your hospital."

Lauren couldn't remain silent any longer. "You two are pure Abbott and Costello." She was smiling radiantly.

"Where do I go now?" asked Paul.

"Drive to the ambulance bay and park. Turn on the lights."

The three of them got out and walked in to the reception desk, where a clerk greeted them.

"What are you bringing us?"

"Nothing, we're here to pick up a patient," Arthur replied in an authoritative voice.

He presented himself as Dr. Brunswick. He had come to take charge of a patient, Lauren Kline, who was scheduled for transfer to an extended-care facility tonight. The nurse on duty asked for the transfer forms, and Arthur handed her a sheaf of papers. Her whole being seemed to frown. "Why on earth did you choose to show up just as we're changing shifts? The transfer will take at least half an hour, and I'm due to go off duty in five minutes."

Arthur apologized: he and the driver had had other patients ahead of this one.

"I'm sorry too." The nurse told them the patient was on the fifth floor, Room 505, and directed them to the elevators. She would sign the paperwork, leave it on the driver's seat in the ambulance, and notify her replacement. This was no time of night for a transfer! Arthur couldn't resist telling her that it was never a good time for a transfer: it was always too early or too late. She ignored his remark.

"I'll get the gurney," said Paul to cut short their exchange. "See you up there, Doctor."

The nurse offered to call an orderly to help. Arthur declined, but asked her if she would be kind enough to leave Lauren's medical records in the ambulance with her other papers.

"The records stay here. A copy will be mailed to you, you should know that." Suddenly she looked suspicious.

"I know that, Miss," said Arthur. "I only need her most recent labs—blood sugar, chem screen, CBC, hematocrit, blood gases."

"Wow! That was really impressive," whispered Lauren. "Where did you pick all that up?"

"TV," Arthur joked back in a low voice.

The nurse told him he could look at the chart in Lauren's room, and offered to take them up there. Arthur thanked her and said she needn't bother—she could leave her shift in five minutes, as planned. They would manage. Paul, who'd just returned with the gurney, hurried Arthur down the corridor. The elevator whisked the three conspirators to the fifth floor. As the doors opened, Arthur said to Lauren, "So far, so good."

"Yes!" Lauren and Paul said in unison.

"You *were* talking to me?" Paul added.

"To both of you."

A young medical student burst out of a room, looking frantic. Catching sight of them, he ran over, peered at Arthur's name tag, and grabbed his elbow. "Dr. Brunswick! Thank God you're here. I need help in 508. Follow me!"

The student ran back to the room he had just left.

"What do we do now?" Arthur asked, in a tone of panic.

"You're asking me?" said Paul, equally terrified.

"No, I'm asking Lauren!"

"Let's go, we've got no choice," said Lauren. "I'll tell you what to do."

"Yes, let's go, we've got no choice," said Arthur aloud.

"What do you mean, let's go? You're not a doctor. Don't you think we should stop this madness before you kill someone?"

"She's going to help us."

"Oh, well, in that case, if she's going to help us!" said Paul, raising his arms. "Lord, why me? Why me?"

All three of them pushed into Room 508. The medical student stood by the bed, a nurse beside him. He said to Arthur in a panic, "He's gone into cardiac arrhythmia, he's an advanced diabetic, I don't know how to reestablish normal rhythm. I'm only in my third year."

"Never fear, Dr. Brunswick is here," Paul muttered under his breath.

Lauren whispered into Arthur's ear, "Tear off the strip coming out of the EKG machine and hold it up so I can read it too."

"Let's have some light here," Arthur said authoritatively. He went around the bed and tore off a long strip of the

EKG tracing. Unrolling it, he turned his back on the others so Lauren could see the tape.

"It's a ventricular arrhythmia. He's useless!"

Arthur repeated the diagnosis word for word: "It's a ventricular arrhythmia. You're useless!"

Paul rolled his eyes, wiping his hand across his forehead.

"I know it's a ventricular arrhythmia, Doctor," said the student, "but what do we do about it?"

"You don't know anything? What do you mean, what do we do about it?" Arthur repeated, stalling for time.

"Ask him what he's already injected," said Lauren.

"What have you injected so far?"

The nurse replied, her tone betraying her exasperation at the medical student's ineptitude, "Nothing! We haven't injected anything, Doctor. We haven't treated the patient at all."

"Tell me what you think we should do," Arthur said, pretending to address the medical student.

"Shit!" yelled Paul. "We're not here to give medical students lessons. Look at that poor guy in the bed, he's turned blue! You're losing him, buster, I mean, Doctor." Paul was beside himself. "San Quentin," he moaned, "next stop San Quentin!"

"Calm down, buddy." Arthur turned to the nurse. "Forgive him, he's new, but he was the only driver available tonight."

"Give him two milligrams of epinephrine, and we'll place a central tract to drain off the fluid. From now it will be tricky, sweetheart," said Lauren.

"Inject two milligrams of epinephrine," Arthur intoned.

"I already have it drawn up, Doctor," said the nurse. "I

was waiting for someone who knew what they were doing to give the order."

"Then we'll place a central catheter," said Arthur, his tone half-questioning, half-commanding. "Do you know how to place a central catheter?" he asked the student.

"Ask the nurse to do it, she'll be delighted. Doctors never let them do any of the good stuff," said Lauren.

"I've never done one," said the student.

"Nurse, you can handle this, right?" said Arthur.

"No, you go ahead, Doctor, it'll save time. I'll prepare it for you straightaway. But thanks for your vote of confidence. Come with me," she said to the medical student, like a mother to a recalcitrant child. "At least you can help with the supplies." The nurse left the room with the med student following sheepishly at her heels.

"What do I do now?" asked Arthur, his voice stifled, panic-stricken.

"We're getting out of here, that's what we do," said Paul. "We're out of here and running, right now!"

Lauren interrupted, "You can do this, Arthur. I'll talk you through it."

As she was speaking, the nurse returned with a tray holding a cardiac needle, catheter, and other supplies.

"Stand over him, aim for two fingers below the sternum—you know where the sternum is, don't you? I'll tell you if you're not in the right place. Hold it at a fifteen-degree angle and then push the needle in, slowly but firmly. If you're in the right place, you'll see clear fluid flow back into the syringe. If you miss, it'll be blood. And pray you have beginner's luck—because if you don't, we're in it up to our ears. Us and the guy lying there."

"I can't do this," Arthur muttered under his breath.

"You have no choice, nor does he. This man is going to die if you don't."

"Did you call me sweetheart, or was I dreaming?"

Lauren smiled. "Go ahead, and take a deep breath before you stick the needle in." The nurse handed the tract tube to Arthur. "Take it by the plastic end, and good luck!" Arthur placed the needle where Lauren had told him. The nurse watched attentively. "That's perfect," murmured Lauren, "tilt it down a little more. Now, in one movement." The needle sank into the patient's thorax. "That's good. Now, turn that little valve on the side of the tube." Arthur did as he was told. An opaque fluid started trickling into the tube.

"Bravo. Done like a pro! You just saved his life!"

Paul had already come close to fainting twice. "I don't believe this," he kept muttering.

The patient's heart, free of the fluid that had been compressing it, resumed a normal beat. The nurse thanked Arthur and said, "I'll take over now." Arthur and Paul made their farewells and went back into the corridor. Paul could not resist poking his head back into the room and calling to the student, "Useless."

Returning to Arthur, he said, "God, you really had me scared there."

"She helped me. She told me what to do."

Paul shook his head. "Any minute now I'm going to wake up, and when I phone to tell you about the nightmare I'm having, you'll laugh. Boy, will you laugh!"

"Come on, Paul, let's do what we came here to do."

They entered Room 505. Arthur pushed the light switch and the fluorescent tubes shimmered into life. Paul went to the bed and looked down at Lauren's body. "You're right, pal, she's a knockout. A little on the pale side, though, almost ghostly, wouldn't you say?"

Arthur laughed. "Okay, enough. Now, wheel the gurney in beside the bed."

Arthur gently lifted Lauren's body behind her back. "Now, get your hands under her knees, and watch out for the IV. We'll lift her on the count of three. One. Two. Three!"

They gently hoisted Lauren's body onto the gurney. Arthur draped blankets over her, unhooked the IV bag from its pole, and looped it over a hook above her head.

"Phase one accomplished. Now let's get back downstairs. No need to hurry, we're just going about our business."

"Yes, Doctor," said Paul, gritting his teeth.

"You guys are doing really well," said Lauren.

As they headed for the elevator, the nurse called to them from the end of the corridor.

Arthur slowly turned around. "Yes, Nurse?"

"Everything's under control here, do you need a hand?"

"No, everything's fine here, too."

"Thanks again, Doctor."

"Don't mention it."

The doors opened and they entered the elevator. Arthur and Paul both gave a sigh of relief.

"Three top models, a couple of weeks in Hawaii, a Ferrari, and a yacht."

"What are you talking about?"

"My fee. I'm just beginning to calculate what you owe me for tonight."

The hall was deserted when they emerged from the elevator. They crossed it with hurried steps and loaded Lauren's body into the back of the ambulance. On Arthur's seat were the transfer papers and a small yellow Post-it note: "Call me tomorrow, there are a couple of blanks that need filling in on the transfer form. See you soon. Karen (415) 555-0700, extension 2154."

The ambulance left Memorial Hospital.

"Actually, body snatching is pretty easy," said Paul.

"I guess not a lot of people want to do it," said Arthur.

"Yeah. I can understand why. Where to now, Doc?"

"First stop, my apartment. And then another place, which is also in a coma; we're going to wake it up."

The ambulance climbed back up Market Street and turned onto Van Ness. The neighborhood was quiet.

Arthur's plan called for an initial detour to transfer Lauren's body from the ambulance to his car. While Paul was returning the "borrowed" vehicle to his stepfather's shop, Arthur would bring down everything he had prepared for the drive and their stay in Carmel. The medical supplies had been carefully wrapped and stored in his refrigerator.

Reaching the apartment building, Paul tried to activate the garage door, but there was no response.

"This is exactly like a bad B movie," Paul said.

"What's the matter?" asked Arthur.

"In a bad B movie you'd drop the polite manner; you'd deliver a line out of the corner of your mouth. 'What the hell's going on?' is what you'd say. Well, in this case, it's your garage door that's not opening. There's an ambulance stolen from my stepfather's garage parked in front of your driveway with a body inside at just the time your neighbors come out to take their dogs for a piss."

"Shit!"

"That about sums it up, Arthur."

"Hand me that remote."

Paul passed it across with a shrug, and Arthur jabbed frantically at the button. Nothing happened.

"On top of it all, he thinks I'm a moron," Paul groaned.

"It must be the battery."

"All geniuses get stung by this kind of detail sooner or later," said Paul sarcastically.

"Paul, go circle the block while I find a new battery."

"Better pray you've got one in the bottom of a drawer somewhere."

"Don't argue, just go on up," said Lauren.

Arthur left the ambulance and raced up the stairs. He looked in the kitchen, the bathroom, the bedroom. By the time Paul was making his fifth circuit, Arthur had ransacked every drawer in the house and still hadn't found a battery.

"I'm dead meat if the cops decide to pull me over," Paul grumbled. As he began his sixth circuit, a patrol car appeared. "I am dead meat!"

The car pulled alongside him; the officer signaled him to lower his window.

"You lost?"

"No, I'm waiting for my partner. He's gone to get some stuff from his apartment, then we're taking Daisy back to the garage."

"Who's Daisy?" asked the policeman.

"This ambulance. It's her last tour of duty, she's done her time, we've been together for ten years, Daisy and me. It's hard to say good-bye, know what I mean? A whole lot of memories, a big piece of my life."

The cop nodded. He understood; he just asked Paul not to take too long. People would start calling in to report him. Folks in this neighborhood were nosy and prone to worry.

"Don't I know it, Officer, I live around here. Good night!"
The officer returned the salute, and the patrol car pulled
away. Inside, the driver bet his partner ten dollars that Paul
wasn't waiting for anyone.

"I bet he can't bring himself to turn in his old lady. Ten
years together, that's a long time."

"Yeah! Funny, though. Most emergency-services guys are
always complaining that the city won't give them the money
for new equipment."

"Yeah, but ten years, you really get attached."

"That's for sure."

Arthur stood in the middle of the living room, racking
his brain for where he might find a battery.

"The TV remote," Lauren said softly.

He spun around to look at her, then grabbed for the little
black device. He tore off its tiny rear flap and removed the
battery, quickly transferring it to the garage-door remote.
Then he ran to the window, leaned out, and pressed the
button.

Paul was beginning his ninth circuit when he saw the
door start to rise. He drove right in, praying that the door
would close faster than it had opened. "It really was the
battery. What a jerk!"

Meanwhile, Arthur hurried down the stairs to the garage.

"Everything okay?"

"For you or for me? Truthfully, I'm ready to strangle you."

"Why don't you help me instead? We still have work
to do."

"I've done nothing but help!"

They carried Lauren's body with great care. They sat her
in the back of Arthur's car, the IV bag hanging from the coat
hook, and wrapped her in a blanket. Her head rested

against the door. Anyone looking inside would assume she was asleep.

"I feel like I'm in a Tarantino movie," grumbled Paul. "You know, I'm the bad guy who gets rid of . . ."

"Shut up, you're going to say something stupid."

"Why? Haven't we done enough stupid things tonight? Are *you* going to take back the ambulance?"

"No, but she's beside you. You'll hurt her feelings."

Lauren put her hand on Arthur's shoulder. "Don't fight. You've both had a hard day," she said, in a calming voice.

"You're right, let's keep things moving."

"I'm right even when I don't say a thing?" Paul grumbled.

"Go to your stepfather's garage and I'll come pick you up in ten minutes. I'm going back up to fetch the equipment."

Paul climbed into the ambulance and left; this time the garage door opened without incident. Crossing Union Street, he failed to notice the same squad car that had stopped him earlier.

"Let a car slip in between us and follow him," said one of the policemen.

The ambulance turned into Van Ness, followed at a short distance by patrol car 627. When Paul drove into the body shop ten minutes later, the police slowed down, then returned to their usual rounds. Paul never even knew he'd been followed.

A quarter hour later, Arthur appeared. Paul came into the street and got into the passenger seat of the Saab.

"You took the scenic route?"

"I drove slowly, because of her."

"And we'll be driving all night?"

"Exactly. You can relax now, Paul. We've almost made it. You've just done me an incredible favor. I know you took some huge risks. It was a lot to ask."

"Just drive. I can't stand thank-yous."

The car left the city heading south on 280. Soon they veered off toward Pacifica and then onto Route 1, the highway leading along the cliffs to Monterey Bay and Carmel. It was the route that Lauren and her old Triumph had been headed for early one morning the previous summer.

The scenery was spectacular. The cliffs made pale lace patterns against the blackness of the night. A waning moon shed its pale glow on the freeway, which, even at this hour, had its lone travelers and trucks. They drove to the sound of the Samuel Barber violin concerto.

Paul was driving now. Arthur stared out into the night. He knew the enormity of what he was doing. At the end of this journey, there would be another awakening—of memories that he had let lie for far too long.

Chapter
TEN

Arthur had studied architecture at the University of California, Berkeley, while living in the small apartment in San Francisco that his mother had bequeathed to him. When he turned twenty-five he sold the apartment and left for Europe. He went to Paris for two great years, attending the Camondo School and living in a studio in the Latin Quarter. Then he studied in Florence for another year before returning to his native California.

Blazoned with diplomas, he landed a job at Miller, a well-known local architecture and design firm, and worked part time at the Museum of Modern Art. He met his friend Paul there, and two years later they started up their own architecture agency. Boosted by a local real-estate boom, their firm acquired a solid reputation, and by now they had more than a dozen employees. Paul looked after construction and the business end of things; Arthur designed furniture and interiors. Each man was comfortable and confident in his role, and in five years of partnership there had never been even a shadow of conflict between them. They were inseparable.

The two of them had a lot in common. They had the same sense of friendship, a taste for living fully, and childhoods charged with similar emotions. Like Paul, Arthur had been brought up by his mother. Paul's father had left his family when Paul was five, and had never come back; Arthur had been three when his father left, to go to Europe. He had been a pilot. *"His plane went up so high in the sky that it got hooked by a star."*

Both of them had been raised in the country. Both had gone to boarding school. Both had grown up without a father.

Lillian, Arthur's mother, was a French poet who had moved to California to marry his father. After her husband's disappearance, she had waited for his return for a long time, and then had seemed to stop mourning. Arthur had spent the first ten years of his life far from the city—by the sea, near Carmel, a delightful little town where Lili (his mother's nickname) owned a house. It was large, in white wood, and overlooked the ocean, and it lay at the top of a vast garden that stretched all the way down to the beach. Anthony, an old friend of Lili's, lived in the guesthouse. He was a painter and Lili had taken him in. He helped her with the house and the upkeep of the grounds, and in the evening he and Lili would talk long into the night. For Arthur, Anthony was a friend and a male presence lacking in his life since his father's disappearance.

Arthur attended the local Monterey school. Anthony dropped him off in the morning; at four, his mother picked him up. They were precious years. His mother was his best friend and she taught him everything the human heart holds dear. Sometimes she woke him up early just to show him a beautiful dawn and to explain how to discern the birdsongs in the cacophony of the breaking day. She taught him the names of every flower in the garden; and how, just from a leaf's design, you could tell the tree whose sap had fed it. She took him around the garden, showing him the places where she had tamed nature, and others where she'd deliberately let it run wild.

During the green and amber seasons, she had him recite the names of the birds that interrupted their long flights to seek rest in the heights of the sequoias. In the vegetable garden, lovingly tended by Anthony, she showed him how to harvest the vegetables that seemed to him to have sprung up by magic—"but pick only the ripe ones." At the water's edge, she had him count the waves that on calm days gently lapped against the rocks, as though seeking forgiveness for their violence in other seasons. She taught him to "inhale the breath of the ocean, its pulse, its changing moods. The sea holds our gaze, just as the land holds our feet." She explained how to forecast coming shifts in the weather by studying the fluctuations of wind and clouds. She was seldom wrong.

Arthur knew every remote inch of their garden; he could have walked it backward with his eyes closed. It held not a single secret. Every burrow in it had a name, just as every animal that chose it for a final resting place had its tomb. But more than anything else, Lili taught him to love to tend the roses. The rose garden was full of magic, a place where a hundred different scents mingled. Lili used to take him there and tell him stories in which children dreamed of being grown-ups, and grown-ups dreamed of being children again. Of all the flowers, roses were her favorites.

One summer morning, at first light, she came into his room, sat on his bed, and stroked his curls. "Come on, sweetheart, or the sun will get there first."

The little boy caught his mother's fingers, squeezed them in his small hand, and laid his cheek against her palm.

Lili's hand had a smell that would never fade from Arthur's memory, a blend of different fragrances that she combined herself and dabbed on her neck each morning while sitting at her dressing table.

"Come on, honey, we'll have to race the sun. Meet me in the kitchen in five minutes."

Arthur stretched, yawned, and pulled on old cotton pants and a heavy gray pullover. He dressed in silence, for his mother had taught him to respect the stillness of dawn. Knowing exactly where they would be going after breakfast, he tugged on his rubber boots. Then he went down to the big kitchen.

"Don't make any noise, you'll wake Anthony."

She'd taught him to like coffee, its taste but especially its smell.

"How are you this morning, sweetheart?"

"Fine."

"So open your eyes and look around. Don't let life pass you by. Think about the colors and the feel of things. Soak it in. When you're a man, you'll remember all this."

"I'm already a man!"

"I mean a grown-up."

"Aren't kids the same as grown-ups?"

"Grown-ups have worries that kids don't. They're not afraid of the same kinds of things."

Adults were frightened of so many things, she explained:

afraid of aging, of dying, afraid of taking risks, of sickness, sometimes even of the clear-eyed look of a child—afraid of being judged.

"Grown-ups get scared because they don't know what's important in life. That's what I'm trying to teach you. Think about all the little things going on right now. You and me, us talking, the sunrise, the smell of coffee."

She got up, picked up their bowls, and put them in the enamel sink. Then she sponged off the tabletop and slid the tiny heap of crumbs into the hollow of her outstretched hand. By the door there was a woven straw basket full of fishing lines. Rolled up in a napkin on top were bread, cheese, and salami. Putting the basket over her arm, Lili took Arthur's hand.

Together they negotiated the path down to the small dock.

"Look at all those little boats, all that color, like flowers bobbing on the sea."

As always, Arthur waded into the sea, unhitched the rowboat from its metal ring, and hauled it to the shore. Lili set her basket down in it, then climbed aboard.

"Okay, start rowing."

They pulled away from the beach, Arthur tugging at the oars. Well before the shoreline was out of sight, he stopped and pulled the oars into the boat. Lili had already taken out the fishing lines and baited several hooks. As usual, though, she had fixed only one line for him; for the next, much to his disgust, he would have to thread the small, wriggling red worm onto the hook with his own fingers. Holding the cork reel steady between his feet on the floorboards, he slipped the nylon thread around his finger and flipped the baited hook over the side. The little lead weight attached to it swiftly dragged it under. If they were in a good spot, he would soon hook a fish.

They were sitting face-to-face. Neither had spoken for a few minutes when Lili suddenly looked straight at him and said in a voice he had never heard before, "Arthur, you know I can't swim—what would you do if I fell in the water?"

"I'd jump in after you," he answered immediately. Lili became angry. "That's plain stupid!" Arthur was stunned by the vehemence of her voice.

"Try to row back to shore alone, that's what you'd do!" Lili was yelling.

"Your life is all that matters, and don't ever forget it. Don't ever play around with that. Promise!"

"I promise," said the child, timidly.

"You see?" she said, more gently now. "You wouldn't jump in after me."

Arthur began to cry. Lili wiped his tears with the back of her finger.

"Sometimes our impulses and desires make us feel power-less. But part of the art of living is knowing how to fight that feeling; because when we're powerless, we get frightened, and then we lose our grip on our intelligence, our common sense, and we become weak. You're going to be scared in lots of ways in your life, Arthur. But always fight back, and don't hesitate for too long. Think, decide, and then act. Don't have doubts. You have to act on your decisions or you'll be un-happy. Every decision you make can become a kind of game that helps you know yourself better and understand the world.

"So move the world, your world! Look at the landscape around you. See how finely carved the coast is—it's like lace. Look at the sun, lighting it with a thousand different colors. Every tree waves at a different speed under the wind. Do you think nature was afraid, when it made so many details, and so much depth? And the most beautiful thing that the earth has given us is what makes us human beings: it's the joy of sharing. People who can't share—it's as if they're missing a limb.

"See, Arthur, this early morning that we're spending together will be engraved in your memory. Later, when I'm not here anymore, you might think back to it. And listen to me—if I fell in the water, you wouldn't jump right in to rescue me, because that would be silly. What you'd do would be this: you'd stretch your arm out to see if you could help me back on board. If you couldn't, and I drowned, you would know that you had tried. You would have peace of mind. You wouldn't have risked dying for nothing, but you'd have done everything you could to save me."

As they rowed back to shore, Lili took the little boy's head in her hands and kissed him.

"Did I make you sad?"

"Yes. And you'll never drown when I'm here to save you. I'll dive into the water, no matter what you say. I can swim well enough to bring you back."

ℒili left the world as elegantly as she had lived in it. On the morning that she died, the little boy stood by his mother's bed.

"Why?"

Anthony, standing beside the bed, said nothing. He looked at the child.

"Why didn't she even say good-bye to me? I've never done anything like that. You're a grown-up—why do grown-ups always lie to children? How could she leave me while I was asleep?"

Sometimes a child looks at you in such a way that you are taken back far in time, in memory, and it is impossible not to answer.

Anthony put his hands on the boy's shoulders. "She couldn't help it. You don't ask death to come: it just comes. Your mother woke up in the middle of the night in terrible pain. She wanted to wait for the sun to rise, but she couldn't, and she quietly fell asleep."

"It's my fault, then. I was sleeping."

"No, it isn't. Of course it isn't, you mustn't look at it that way. Do you want to know the real reason she left without saying good-bye? Your mother was a great lady, and all great ladies know how to go with dignity, leaving those they love to get on with their lives."

The boy looked straight into Anthony's sorrowful eyes and felt close to him in a way he hadn't before. His eyes followed as a tear rolled down the man's cheek and wound its way through the stubble on his chin. Anthony brushed his eyes with the back of his hand.

"Well, as you can see, I'm crying. Go ahead. You can too: tears wash away the pain."

"I'll cry later," said the boy. "The pain makes me feel close to her. I want to keep it."

"No, little man, you've got your life ahead of you. Don't live in the past. That's what she was trying to teach you—dreams have a price. The pain you are feeling is the price of the dreams she gave you."

"That's a high price, Anthony," the boy said. "Please leave me alone with her."

"You are alone with her. You can close your eyes and

forget I'm here. You're alone with yourself, and it's a long road that lies ahead of you."

"She's beautiful, isn't she? I thought death would be scary, but she's beautiful."

The child looked at his mother's hand, the blue veins under the soft, clear skin. He took it to his lips and slowly stroked his cheek with it before kissing her palm.

No man's kiss could rival that tenderness.

"I love you," said the boy. "I've always loved you as a child, but now I'm a man, and I'll love you forever."

"Arthur?" said Anthony.

"Yes."

"She left a letter for you."

Anthony handed Arthur an envelope. "I'll leave you alone now."

Arthur sniffed the heavy, cream-colored paper and inhaled his mother's scent before he unsealed it.

My darling Arthur,

When you read this letter, I know that, deep down, you'll be angry at me for playing this dirty trick on you. Sweetheart, this is the last letter I will ever write you, the last will and testament of my love.

My spirit is taking flight, carried up high by all the happiness you've given me. Life is wonderful, Arthur; it's when you find it tiptoeing away from you that you realize it. So you must remember to embrace it every day. Sometimes life brings us low, but you must never let yourself give up. Since the day you were born I've seen that special light in your eyes which makes you different from all the other children. I've seen you fall and get up with your teeth clenched, when any other boy would have cried and given up. You're brave, and that makes you strong. But it might also make you weak. Feelings are made to be shared, and strength and courage can be turned against you if you don't make proper use of them. Men get to cry too, Arthur; men also feel pain.

From now on I won't be around to guide you. The time has come for you to become a man. It will be a long journey.

Never lose sight of your child's soul. Never lose sight of your dreams, because your dreams will be the goals that shape your life, the taste and the smell that makes you want to get up and discover each new morning. Soon you'll encounter another kind of love, not like the love you have for me. When the time comes, share that with someone who will love you, too. When you share a dream—that's when it flowers. Solitude is a garden where the flowers have no scent, and the spirit withers.

Love is wonderful. Remember: you have to give to receive; and you have to be true to yourself if you are to love someone else truly. My strong, brave boy, always trust your instincts, and be faithful to your conscience and your feelings. Live your life to the full. You only have one. Be worthy, share your love, and don't lose the look that you had in your eyes on those mornings when we woke up to share the dawn. Remember the hours we spent pruning roses together, looking at the moon, learning the smells of flowers, listening to the sounds of the house. Remember how to recognize simple, magical moments like those, and don't let bitter people make them less precious for you. The most important thing I have tried to give you is a sense of wonder. It will give savor to the long journey that lies ahead of you now.

My sweet little man, I must leave you. Hold on tight to this beautiful earth of ours. I love you, my darling. You were my reason for living. And I know how much you love me. I'm leaving with my mind at rest. And I'm proud of you.

Your Mommy.

The little boy folded the letter and put it in his pocket. He kissed his mother's cold forehead. He left the room with a firm step, as she had always taught him: A man who leaves must never look back.

He went into the garden—the dew was still freshly wet—and knelt down by the rosebushes. He spoke to them. "She's gone, she'll never see you again. If only you could understand. My arms feel so heavy."

The rosebushes bowed in the wind, in a flurry of petals. Then, and only then, did he let free his tears, in the rose garden. Anthony watched from the porch.

"Oh, Lili, you left too soon for him," he murmured. "Much too soon. He's alone now—you were the only person he ever let into his world. If there's anything you can do now—from wherever you are—then help him open up."

A crow cawed loudly at the bottom of the garden.

"Ah, no, Lili, not that. I'm not his father," Anthony said.

*I*t was the longest day Arthur ever lived through. Late that evening, Arthur and Anthony were sitting together on the porch, deep in thought, surrounded by the memories that saturated those walls, when Arthur began hearing a kind of music in his head. It was soft at first—a sort of singing, with words that sounded like his mother's voice.

"Anthony?"

"Yes, Arthur."

"She gave me her music."

And finally the child fell asleep, in Anthony's arms.

Anthony sat motionless for a long time with Arthur's head cradled on his shoulder, for fear of waking the child. When he was sure the boy was sound asleep, he took him in his arms and walked back into the house. Lili had been gone only a few hours, and already the atmosphere was changing. A subtle resonance, and certain smells and colors, seemed to be drawing back, preparing to vanish altogether.

*L*ili had seen to everything before she went. A few weeks after her death, Anthony closed up most of the large house, keeping only the two first-floor rooms open; there he would live out his days. He drove Arthur to the station and put him on a train that carried him off to a boarding school. Arthur grew up there, alone. It was a nice place, well run and comfortable; the teachers were respected, even liked, by the students. Certainly Lili could not have picked a better school for him. Nothing seemed sad there, on the face of it. But when he entered it, Arthur took with him his memories of his mother, and they filled every available space in his head. He learned to keep living. Using bits and pieces of Lili's teachings, he put together attitudes, gestures, an implacably logical mind. Arthur had been an even-tempered child, and he remained so as a teenager, adding to that an unusually acute flair for observation. The young man never seemed to agonize over anything. He was an ordinary student, neither brilliant nor a dunce, his grades always above average (except in history, in which he excelled); and he progressed naturally through to graduation.

One June evening at the end of his school years, he received a summons from the school principal. She told him that his mother, knowing she was ill, had come to see her a year before her death. They had spent hours working out all the details of Arthur's education. Lili had given the principal, Mrs. Senard, the keys to the Carmel house where he had grown up, and also to a little apartment she had purchased in town. The apartment had been rented out to tenants until the month before he turned eighteen. The rent had been transferred to an account in his name, along with Lili's savings. There was more than enough to finance him through college.

Arthur took the keys from the desk where Mrs. Senard had set them down. The ring had a small silver ball with a groove down the middle, fastened with a tiny clasp. Arthur pushed back its little lever and the ball opened. In each half was a miniature photo: one of himself when he was seven, the other of Lili. Arthur carefully snapped the ring shut.

"What do you plan to study?"

"Architecture."

"Will you go back to the house in Carmel?"

"No, not yet. Not for a long time."

"Why?"

"She knows. It's a secret."

The principal rose to signal that the meeting was over. As they walked to her office door, she took him in her arms and held him tight. She slipped an envelope into his hand and closed his fingers over it.

"This is also from her," Mrs. Senard said quietly. "It's for you. She asked me to give it to you when you finished school."

As soon as she opened the door to her office, Arthur was out and walking down the corridor without looking back. He held the long, heavy keys in one hand and the letter in the other. She watched as he turned the corner, and then closed the two heavy doors of her office.

Chapter
ELEVEN

*T*he car was approaching the final minutes of this long night's drive. Its headlamps lit up the lines alternating between curves that had been blasted out of the rock cliffs and straight stretches flanked on either side by marshland and empty beaches. Lauren was dozing. Paul drove in silence, focused on the road and deep in his own thoughts. Arthur took advantage of this peaceful moment to remove a letter unobtrusively from his pocket. It was the one he had placed there along with the heavy keys from the writing desk in his apartment.

When he opened the envelope a waft of fragrance escaped, laden with memories. It was a blend of the two perfumes his mother used to concoct in a big yellow crystal flask with a tarnished silver stopper. The smell released his own memories of her. He removed the letter and carefully unfolded it.

My darling Arthur,

If you are reading these words, it means you've finally made up your mind to set out for Carmel. How I'd love to know how old you are right now.

You're holding the keys to the house where we spent such wonderful years together. I knew you wouldn't go there right away, that you'd wait until you felt ready to reawaken the old place.

Soon you'll be pushing open the front door. I can hear its creak now. Every room you walk into will stir memories. You'll open up the shutters one by one, letting in the sunlight that I shall miss so much. And of course you'll go to the rose garden. Walk softly up to the roses. Surely by now they will have run wild.

You should also go to my study. Make yourself comfortable there. In the closet you'll find my small black suitcase. Open it, if you wish; if you have the strength. Inside you'll find notebooks full of the pages I wrote to you every day of your childhood.

Your life is ahead of you. You alone are master of it. Be worthy of all the things I loved.

I love you, wherever I am, and I'm watching over you. Your mother, Lili.

Discreetly he returned the letter to his pocket.

*A*rthur gave Paul directions from the passenger seat. It had been more than twenty years since he'd been here, and yet nothing had changed; he recognized the smell of the place, even in the dead of night. Arthur saw the cypress that stood herald at the turn onto the dirt road, potholed by winter rains and baked by summer suns. As they rounded a bend Arthur caught sight of the ornate, green wrought-iron gate that protected the property.

"Here we are," said Arthur.

"Got the keys?"

"I'll open the gate and let you through." Arthur got out of the car and inhaled the fresh, cold sea air. "You go on down to the house and wait for me. I'll walk."

"Is she coming with you or staying in the car?"

Arthur leaned in the window and said in a forthright voice, "It's time you talked to her directly."

"I'd rather not."

"I'll let you stay by yourself, alone," Lauren said gently. "I think that's best for the moment."

"You just got lucky, she's staying with you," Arthur told Paul with a grin.

The car pulled away, trailing dust. Arthur stood there quietly for a long time, taking in the dark landscape. Broad strips of ocher-colored soil were bordered by umbrella and Monterey pines that Anthony had planted when Arthur was a boy, and which now towered above him. The ground was strewn with pine needles, and in the distance he could hear the ocean. He started down the little stone steps beside the path. Halfway down, he could just make out the remains of the rose garden on his right. The plot was completely over-grown, and a multitude of varied scents rose from the ground, bringing new memories with every step.

As he passed, the cicadas grew briefly silent. The great trees bowed in the slight morning breeze. A few waves broke on the rocks. Before him, the house seemed to be sleeping, as in a fairy tale, or a dream. It seemed smaller; the walls had been damaged slightly, but the roof was intact.

The shutters were closed. Paul had parked by the wide front porch and was waiting for Arthur beside the car. "You took your time getting here!"

"More than twenty years."

"So? What now?" Paul asked.

They would first need to put Lauren's body in his mother's study on the ground floor. Arthur slipped the key in the lock and unhesitatingly turned it the wrong way, which was the right way to open it. Some lessons become automatic, even when not repeated for years. The click of the latch prompted instant recognition, as if he had heard it just the day before. He walked into the hallway and opened the first door on the left. He unfastened the shutters, deliberately ignoring his surroundings. There would be time enough to rediscover this place, and he would relish it properly when that time came. Arthur and Paul rapidly unpacked the boxes, laid Lauren's body on the sofa bed, and put the intravenous drip back in place. Arthur pushed the shutters back again, leaving them just slightly ajar. Then he picked up a little brown box and told Paul to come to the kitchen. "I'll make us coffee; open the box while I'm getting things ready."

Arthur opened the kitchen cabinet, took out a small Italian espresso maker, and set it on the stove. He found an old, unopened can of coffee in the cupboard and spooned some out.

"A French mother with an Italian coffeepot?" Paul asked. "How do you use that thing, anyway?"

"It was her only concession to the Italians." Arthur explained how the contraption worked. You put two or three tablespoons of good coffee in a little sieve, and you placed that between the bottom half of the pot, which you filled with water, and the top half. You screwed the compartments together, and you put the whole thing on the flame. When the water boiled, it rose up to the coffee grains in the little sieve and pushed through them into the top part, filtered only by a fine metal grille. There was no paper filter; this way, the aroma of the ground coffee beans was captured more effectively. But you had to take the pot off the flame in time, so the top part didn't boil—"Nothing worse than boiled coffee."

When he finished, Paul whistled. "You need to be an engineer around here to get a coffee."

"You need to be better than that, pal—you need talent. It's a ceremony."

Paul grimaced doubtfully. Before turning on the burner, Arthur bent down and opened the tap on the butane tank under the sink.

"You think there's still gas in that bottle?" asked Paul.

"Anthony would never have left the house with an empty tank in the kitchen, and I'll bet you there are at least two more full ones in the garage."

Without thinking, Paul got up to flick the light switch by the door, and the room flooded with yellow light.

"How come there's electricity?"

"I called the company Friday and asked them to reconnect us. Same for the water, in case you're worried. But turn it off; we'll have to dust the lightbulbs first, or they'll explode when they get hot."

"Where'd you learn all this, dusting lightbulbs, making Italian coffee?"

"Here, in this room. And a lot of other stuff too."

"What about my coffee?"

Arthur set two cups on the wooden tabletop and poured out the fragrant liquid. "Give it a moment."

"Why?"

"Because you'll burn yourself, and anyway, you have to inhale it first. Let the aroma flood your nostrils."

"Cut the crap about the coffee. Let the aroma flood my nostrils? You're driving me crazy."

Paul raised the cup to his lips and instantly spat his tiny sip of hot black liquid back into his cup. Just then Lauren came and stood behind Arthur and whispered, "I like this place. I feel good here, it's soothing."

"Where were you?"

"Looking around, while you gave a lecture on coffee."

"You talking to her again?" Paul interrupted, irascibly.

Ignoring his friend completely, Arthur said to Lauren, "And do you like it?"

"Anyone would," she answered. "But there are secrets here. The place is full of them—I can feel them in the walls."

"If you find my presence intrusive, just pretend I'm not here," Paul said sarcastically.

With a glimmer in her eye, Lauren whispered to Arthur that she longed to be alone with him. She couldn't wait for him to show her around. She added that they needed to talk. He asked what about.

"About here. About this. About yesterday."

Paul, waiting testily for Arthur to turn his attention from Lauren back to him, broke in, "Do you still need me? Because if not, I'm heading out now. You know your little talks with Ghostie make me feel uncomfortable."

"Don't be so closed-minded."

"You want me to be more open-minded. Me, the guy who stole an ambulance to help you steal a body from a hospital one fine Sunday night. The guy who's now drinking Italian coffee, hours from home, without a wink of sleep. You don't think I'm open-minded? You've got a lot of nerve!"

"That's not what I meant."

Paul didn't know what Arthur had meant, nor did he care: he would go back to the city before the yelling started—"It would be a pity to fight now, after everything we've been through." Arthur was concerned that his friend might be too tired to drive all the way back that night. But Paul reassured him: thanks to that Italian coffee (he insisted ironically on the term), he was good for at least twenty hours nonstop before the Sandman would come anywhere near him.

"Now, is it all right for me to leave you and the ghost and the body all here alone, without a car, in a deserted house in the middle of the night?" Paul asked.

"Actually there should be a vintage Ford station wagon in the garage, an old woody."

"When was the last time anyone drove it?"

"I guess it's been a while."

"And you think 'Woody' will start?"

"It'll be okay as soon as I recharge the battery. Don't worry about me."

"Sure, you'll recharge the battery, just like that. Of course I'll worry about you. Under normal circumstances, if you were alone in this house I'd be worried about ghosts. But of course you brought your own."

"Go on."

Paul started the car and lowered his window. "You're sure you'll be all right?"

"I'll be fine."

"Okay, then I'm off."

"Paul?"

"Yes?"

"I mean it, thanks for everything."

"It was nothing."

"It was a hell of a lot. You took all those risks for me without knowing the whole picture, all out of loyalty and friendship, and I know it."

"I know you know. Okay, I'm out of here before we start getting sentimental. Take good care of yourself and keep me posted at the office."

Arthur promised and watched until the Saab's taillights faded from view. Lauren came out and stood beside him.

"So?" she said. "Will you show me around?"

"Which first, house or garden?"

"Before we begin, where are we?"

"Lili's house."

"Who's Lili?"

"Lili was my mother, and this is where I grew up."

"Has she been gone for long?"

"A long time."

"And you've never been back here?"

"Never. You're not the only ghost in my life," he said gently.

"It's difficult for you, isn't it, being here?"

"That's not quite the word; let's say it's important for me to be here."

"And you did this for me?"

"I did it because it was time to try."

"To try what?"

"I forgot you had such a stubborn streak." He paused. "To open a little black suitcase."

"What are you talking about?"

"Undiscovered memories."

"You have a lot of them here?"

"This was my mother's home, and mine, too, for a while."

"Did your mother die suddenly?"

"No, she died of cancer; she knew all about it ahead of time. But for me it was very sudden. Come on, I'll show you around the garden."

The two of them went down the front steps, and Arthur led Lauren to the ocean. They sat on the rocks at the water's edge, shaded by a straggling, windblown cypress.

"I spent so many hours sitting here with her—I used to count the waves, making bets with myself. We often came down to watch the sunset. Lots of people from around here gather on the beaches for a half hour in the evening to watch it. Every night it's different. Because of the temperature of the ocean, the air—lots of factors—the colors of the sky at sunset are never exactly the same. In cities, people watch the evening news; here, people watch the sunset. It's a ritual."

"Did you live here long?"

"Until I was ten. That's when she died."

"Tonight you'll show me the sunset."

"In this neck of the woods, it's a must," he said with a smile.

Behind them, the house was beginning to shine in the early-morning light. The facade was a little wind-beaten on the seaward side, but overall it had stood up well over the years. From the outside no one would have believed it had been sleeping so long.

"It's in pretty good shape," said Lauren.

"Anthony was a meticulous caretaker. He was a gardener, a repairman, a fisherman, a baby-sitter. He was an unknown painter who turned up here one day, and my mother took him in. He lived in the little outbuilding. He was a friend of both my parents, but I believe he was always in love with my mother, even when my father was still alive. I suspect they ended up as lovers, but much later on. She helped him live, and he helped her mourn. They didn't talk much—at least while I was awake—but they were close. They understood each other's thoughts. They healed themselves together. The calm between them was almost disconcerting. It was as if they'd vowed to avoid ever feeling anger."

"What happened to him?"

Anthony had outlived Lili by ten years. He had retreated into the very study where Lauren's body now lay. He spent the last years of his life looking after the house, and died early one winter. One cool, bright morning he woke up feeling weary. As he was oiling the gate hinges, he felt a dull twinge in his chest. He walked among the trees gasping for air, which all of a sudden seemed in short supply. The lower boughs of the old pine under which he had spent his spring and summer siestas caught him in its branches when he fell helplessly over. He crawled to the house, in pain, and called the neighbors for help. He was taken to the hospital in Monterey, where he died a few days later. At his death, the family attorney contacted Arthur to ask him what should be done with the house.

"The attorney told me that he was amazed when he went to see the house. Anthony left everything in perfect order, as if he had been about to go on a trip the day he had his attack."

"Maybe that's what he had in mind?"

"Anthony, go on a trip? Just going to Carmel for grocery shopping was an expedition. No, I believe he had the dying elephant's instinct: he felt his hour coming, or else maybe he'd had enough and just gave up."

To explain what he meant, Arthur told Lauren about what his mother had said one day, when he asked her about death. He had wanted to know if grown-ups were afraid of it. He remembered her reply word for word: *"When you've had a really good day, when you've risen early in the morning to go fishing and you've been running around or working in the rose garden with Anthony, by evening you're worn out, right? And then, even though you usually hate going to bed, all you want to do is dive into those sheets. On evenings like those you're not scared to go to sleep. Life is a bit like that. When you've had a rich and full life, when your body is slowing down and everything's becoming a bit more difficult, and tiring, the thought of going to sleep forever doesn't scare you the way it used to."*

"Mom was already sick when she said that. I think she knew what she was talking about."

"What did you answer?"

"I grabbed her arm tight and asked her if she was 'worn out,' and she smiled. Anyway, all this is just to explain that I think Anthony had reached some state of wisdom."

"Like the elephants," Lauren said softly.

As if with one mind, they both rose and crossed back toward the house. Arthur abruptly left the path, went over to the blue wooden gate, and opened it slowly.

"Now for the heart of the kingdom."

"Why the heart of the kingdom?"

"This was the center of everything. Lili was mad about roses."

It was the only subject he had ever seen his mother and Anthony squabble about. "Mom knew every flower personally. If you dared cut just one of them, she would realize it at once." The garden had a staggering variety. Lili had ordered cuttings from catalogs, and took pride in growing hybrids from all over the world, especially ones that were theoretically unsuited to the local climate. She liked challenging the rules.

Arthur had counted no fewer than 135 different varieties in the garden. During one torrential rainstorm, his mother and Anthony had gotten up in the dead of night, raced to the garage, and hauled out a tarpaulin that must have been thirty feet across and a hundred feet long. Anthony had hastily fastened three sides of the tarpaulin to heavy posts. As for the fourth side, they had held it up at arm's length, one standing on a stepladder, the other perched on a tennis umpire's tall chair. They had spent the night there, shaking this giant umbrella whenever it became weighted down with rain. The storm had lasted more than three hours. "I'm convinced they would have been less excited if the house had caught fire. Next morning they looked like two human shipwrecks. But they saved the rose garden."

"There are still dozens of them," Lauren said.

"Oh, but these are wild roses, the ones you can see now. They'll grow no matter what happens. You'd better wear gloves if you want to cut any, the thorns are vicious."

They spent a good part of the day discovering and rediscovering the house's surroundings. Arthur pointed out the tree he'd carved his name in, and he showed Lauren where he had broken his collarbone, falling from a pine.

"How could you have done that?"

"I was ripe, I fell out of the tree."

The day passed without either of them even realizing it. As sunset approached, they returned to the ocean's edge, sat on a rock, and contemplated the spectacle that people gathered from far away to see. When night fell they retreated to the house, and Arthur gave Lauren's body a sponge bath. Then he ate a light supper, and they settled down by the fire he had made in the little living room.

"Well now, what about this black suitcase?"

"Nothing escapes you, does it?"

"I listen, that's all."

"It's a case that belonged to Mom. She kept all her letters and souvenirs in it. In fact, I believe it probably holds everything that mattered in her life."

"What do you mean, you *believe*?"

The case had always been a great mystery, he said. He could go anywhere in the house, except for the closet where she kept it. Opening that was strictly forbidden. "And believe me, I'd never have risked it!"

"Where is it?"

"In the study next door."

"And you never came back to open it. I can't believe it!"

He had never wanted to rush this moment. His mother's whole life must be in there. He had waited until he could feel that he was truly a grown-up, ready to take the risk of finding out what was inside and having to understand it. Seeing Lauren's skeptical frown, he confessed, "Okay, the fact is I was always scared to open it."

"Scared of what?"

"I don't know, scared it would change my image of her. Scared of feeling pain."

"Go get it!"

Arthur did not move. Lauren insisted: there was no reason to be afraid. Lili had packed her whole life into a case because she had wanted her son to discover one day who she really was. "What are you afraid of—passing judgment on your mother? You're not that kind of person. You can't ignore what's in the suitcase: you'd be breaking her rules. She left it to you so that you could learn all about her, things that death didn't let you two share. So that you could really know her—not just as a child, but with the eyes and the heart of a grown man."

For a few seconds Arthur considered what Lauren had just said. Keeping his eyes on her, he got up, went out to the study, and opened the closet. The small black case sat on the shelf in front of him. Taking a firm grip on its worn handle, he took a deep breath and pulled all of this past into the present. Returning to the little living room, he sat down cross-legged next to Lauren. Glancing over at her, Arthur snapped the locks, and the lid opened. The case was overflowing with letters, photos, and bits of memorabilia from Arthur's past: a small plastic model airplane he'd made to mark a long-gone Mother's Day, a clay ashtray, a seashell necklace—even Arthur's silver baby spoon and shoes. On the very top of the case was a folded letter, stapled shut, on which Lili had written ARTHUR in big letters. He picked it up and unsealed it.

Dearest Arthur,

Here you are, in your house. Time heals all wounds, even though it doesn't spare us a few scars. In this suitcase, you'll find all my memories: memories of you, memories of my life before you, and things I could never tell you about before, because you were a child. You'll see your mother with new eyes. I was your mother and I was also a woman, with fears, and doubts, and failures, and regrets, and also triumphs. So much of the advice I gave you came from the mistakes I made. Parents are like mountains we spend our lives trying to climb, not realizing that one day we ourselves will be those mountains.

There's nothing more complex than raising a child. You spend your whole life giving what you think is best, knowing that you constantly make mistakes. Most parents do it all out of love, even though they are sometimes selfish. On the day I shut this little case I was afraid of disappointing you. I left too soon for you to judge me with an adult's eyes. I don't know how old you'll be when you read this letter. I see you as a handsome young man of about thirty, maybe a little more. God, how I wish I could have spent all these years by your side. I feel so empty when I think that I will never see you again as your eyes open in the morning, never again hear the sound of your voice calling for me. The thought hurts me even more than the illness that is taking me so far away from you.

I always loved Anthony. We never lived as lovers, because I was afraid—afraid of your father, afraid of hurting him, afraid of destroying what I had built, afraid of admitting to myself that I had made a mistake. I was afraid to disturb the established order of things and start all over again—afraid that it wouldn't work, that it was all just a dream. But not owning up to my love for Anthony was a nightmare. Night and day I thought about him, but I didn't let myself give in. After your father died, the fear continued—fear of betrayal and fear of hurting you.

Anthony loved me the way every woman dreams of being loved at least once in her life. But because I was a coward, I never loved him back. I made excuses for my

*weakness, I wallowed in my cheap melodrama, and all
the time I failed to realize that my life was passing me by
at top speed. Your father was a fine man, but to me
Anthony was unique. No one looked at me the way he
did, no one spoke to me the way he did; nothing could
happen to me while I was by his side, and I feared
nothing. He understood all my needs, all my desires,
and never ceased to try to fulfill them. His whole life was
rooted in harmony, gentleness, the gift of giving, whereas I
sought out battles. I made conflict my reason for being. I
knew nothing about the gift of receiving. I forced myself to
believe that such happiness was impossible, that real life
could not possibly be so sweet. One night when you were
about five years old, we made love. I became pregnant but
did not keep the child. I never told him, yet I'm sure he
knew. He guessed everything about me.*

*Perhaps that was for the best, because of what's
happening to me now. But I also believe that this illness
might not have developed if I had been at peace with
myself. We lived all those years in the shadow of my lies:
I cheated life, and life could not forgive me. You see, you
already know a lot more about your mother.*

*I hesitated to tell you all this—once again I feared
your judgment—but haven't I taught you that the worst
lies are the ones we tell ourselves? There are many things
I would have liked to share with you, but we didn't have
enough time. It was because of me, because of my
enormous ignorance, that Anthony did not raise you.
When I knew I was sick it was too late to start over
again.*

*You'll find all sorts of things in this motley bag I'm
leaving you—photos of you, of Anthony, his letters (don't*

*read them, they belong to me; they're here because I can't
bring myself to part with them). You'll be wondering why
there are no photos of your father. I tore them up one
night in a fit of anger and frustration—anger toward
myself . . .*

*I tried my best, my love. I did the best this woman
could do, with all her virtues and defects. But I want you
to know that you were my whole life, my whole reason for
living, the best, most beautiful, most important thing
that ever happened to me. I pray that you will one day
experience what it is to have a child. It will help you
understand many things.*

*My greatest pride will always be that I was your
mother, for always.*

I love you.

Lili

He folded the letter and replaced it on top of the case's
contents. Lauren saw that he was crying. She moved closer
to him and wiped his eyes with her finger. He looked up in
surprise, all his pain washed away by the tenderness of her
gaze. She let her finger drop to his chin. In turn, he laid his
hand on her cheek, then around the nape of her neck,
bringing her face close to his. As soon as their lips brushed
lightly, she pulled away.

"Why are you doing this for me, Arthur?"

"Because I love you."

He took her by the hand and led her outside the house.

"Where are we going?" she asked.

"To the ocean."

"No. Here." She stepped in front of him and unbuttoned
his shirt.

"But how did you—? I thought you couldn't—"

"Don't ask questions. I don't know how I did it."

She let his shirt slide down over his shoulders and ran her hands across his back. He felt at a loss: how do you undress a ghost? Lauren smiled, closed her eyes, and was instantly naked.

There on the porch, she wrapped herself around him and kissed him.

Lauren's spirit was caught up within his body, entering into him for the time of an embrace, as fleeting and magical as an eclipse.

The suitcase was open.

Part
THREE

Chapter
TWELVE

*I*nspector Pilger found the report waiting on his desk when he arrived at work. A supervisor from Memorial Hospital had called police headquarters at eight AM, just after arriving for her shift. A patient in a coma had vanished from the hospital. It appeared to be a kidnapping.

He cursed. "What did I do to you to deserve this, first thing on a Monday morning?" he grumbled at Nathalie, the dispatcher.

"You could at least have shaved, considering it's the beginning of the week," she countered, with a broad but guilty smile.

"That's an interesting reply," he said, stroking his two-day growth. It was true, he should have shaved. He was only two months away from retirement, and already he was neglecting his appearance. "I hope you like that swivel chair you're sitting in, sweetheart, because you're not going to be promoted out of it for a long, long time."

"You're a pillar of cordiality, George. They should build a statue to you."

"Sure thing. Then I can finally decide which pigeons get to shit on me."

Bad start to the week, on the heels of the bad week that had ended only two days before.

For Pilger, a good week was made up of days when cops were called out only to settle neighborhood disputes or enforce respect for the civil laws. The very existence of the Criminal Justice division should make no sense, since it implied that there were people twisted enough in this city to kill, rape, and steal—or even to kidnap a comatose patient from a hospital. He would have liked to think that after thirty years on the job he had seen everything, but every week seemed to yield some new example of human depravity.

"Nathalie!" he bellowed from his office.

"Yes, George?" she replied, her eyes glued to her work. "So, you had a bad weekend?"

"Feel like getting me some doughnuts from downstairs?"

"Nope."

"Oh, come on. I'm not going to be here much longer."

Nathalie was entering reference numbers for the night's reports in the appropriate spaces, but because the boxes were too small and because the head of the Seventh Precinct (her "superior," as she ironically referred to him) was a stickler for detail, she was painstakingly writing in tiny letters, careful not to overshoot the lines. Without lifting her head, she replied, "George, the only way I'd get you doughnuts was if you were retiring tonight."

He jumped up from his chair and came to stand behind her. "Now that's hitting below the belt."

"Hey, I thought that's where you liked it."

"Know where I'm going to put those doughnuts, ducky?"

"I'm a chick. Not a duck."

"You're a ducky, and an ugly one that can't even fly. Strangely, however, you're my kind of duck. Chick. Whatever."

"Go away. This bird is working."

"Oh, c'mon, why don't you put on your grandma's sweater and we'll go downstairs for coffee."

"And who's going to dispatch the calls?"

"Sit tight. Watch this."

He walked over to the rookie stacking files at the far end of the room, grabbed his arm, and steered him across to the desk just inside the front door.

"There you go, tiger, you sit on this nice swivel chair with armrests and coasters." George then pointed to Nathalie. "The lady here has just been promoted to a barstool. You can swivel in this, but no more than two turns in the same direction. When the phone makes a noise, you pick it up and say, 'Good morning, Seventh Precinct, Detective Bureau.' Then you listen, you note everything down on one of these pads, and you don't leave to take a leak until we get back. If anyone asks where Nathalie is, tell them she's having female problems and was last seen running for the pharmacy. Think even you can handle it?"

"If it gets me out of going for coffee with you, I'll even scrub the john, Inspector!"

Pilger ignored the remark, grabbed Nathalie's arm, and hustled her down the stairs.

"Well, your grandma must have looked great in that sweater," he said, studying her with a grin.

"I'm going to be so bored when they finally shove you out the door, George!"

On the corner of the building opposite, a fifties-style sign traced in red neon the outlines of a martini glass with an olive in it. Spelling out the name of the Finzy Bar in glowing blue letters above the cocktail glass, the neon shed a halo of pastel light on the old bar's windows. The Finzy's days of glory were long past. All that remained were yellowed walls and ceilings, time-worn wooden surfaces, aged floorboards hollowed out by thousands of drunken footsteps and the stumblings of one-night lovers. From across the street the place looked like an Edward Hopper painting. Pilger loved the Finzy Bar; it felt like home to him.

He took Nathalie's arm, led her across the street, pulled two stools up to the ancient wooden bar, and ordered two lattes.

"Was your weekend really that bad, you big ape?"

"Sweetheart, if you only knew how dull my weekends are. I'm bored shitless."

"Was it because I couldn't have brunch with you on Sunday?"

He nodded.

"Well, why didn't you go to a museum or something? Get out of the house."

"First thing that happens when I go to museums is I catch a pickpocket red-handed, and bingo, there I am back at the precinct."

"Go to the movies, then."

"I bust some underage kids sneaking into an R-rated flick."

"Then take a walk."

"Now there's an idea, I can go for a walk. That way I

won't look like an asshole wandering down the street. 'So, what's up?' 'Nothing, I'm walking.' Yup, great way to spend your weekend. How's it going with your new boyfriend?"

"Nothing special, but he helps pass the time."

"You know what a man's weak point is?" George asked.

"No, what *are* a man's weak *points*?"

"Men get bored too easily, thrown off track. But I can't see how any man could be bored with a girl like you. If I were fifteen years younger, I'd write my name on all your dance cards."

"But you're fifteen years younger than you think, George."

"Do I take that as a come-on?"

"It's a compliment; at least that's something."

After they finished their lattes, Nathalie rose. "Now, I have work to do and you have to get to the hospital. They sounded frantic."

*W*hen he reached Memorial Hospital, George introduced himself to Head Nurse Jarkowiszski. She looked him up and down, from his unshaven face to his slightly pudgy but nonetheless still somehow elegant physique.

"It's terrifying," she said. "Nothing like this has ever happened before."

In the same overwrought manner, she told him that the chairman of the hospital board was extremely upset. She was sure he'd want to see the inspector that afternoon, before reporting back to the board early in the evening. "You will get her back for us, won't you, Inspector?"

"Maybe, if you start by telling me everything from the beginning."

Jarkowiszski told him the kidnapping had undoubtedly

taken place during the shift change. No one had yet been able to contact the nurse who had been on duty, but the night nurse confirmed that the bed was empty when she had made her rounds at approximately two AM. She had assumed that the patient had died and that the room had not yet been reassigned, following the traditional practice of leaving a bed unoccupied for twenty-four hours following a patient's death. Not until Jarkowiszski had made her first rounds had she realized that something was awry.

"Did you ever think that maybe she woke from her coma and was fed up with this hotel and went for a walk? Natural enough when you've been in bed so long."

"I appreciate your wit, Inspector, but why don't you share it with her mother? She's with one of our administrators right now, but she'll be here any minute."

"Yes, sure." Pilger stared at his toe caps. "If it's a kidnapping, what would anyone stand to gain?"

"What does that matter?" Jarkowiszski answered irritably, as though they were wasting precious time.

"You know," he said, looking at her hard, "strange though it may seem, ninety-nine percent of crimes have a motive. Meaning that, in theory, you don't lift a comatose patient from a hospital on a Sunday night just for a laugh. And incidentally, you're sure she hasn't just been moved to another department?"

"I'm certain of it. The transfer documents are in reception. She was taken away in an ambulance."

"What company?" he asked, taking out his pencil.

"That's what's so odd. There isn't one."

She explained that when she'd come to work that morning, she had not immediately suspected a kidnapping. Informed that Room 505 was free, she had gone straight to

the reception desk to complain. She considered it unacceptable for a transfer to be authorized without first informing
her. "But these days, you know, respect for your superiors?
Anyway, that's not the problem." The receptionist had
shown her the documents, and she had seen at once that
something was wrong. One form was missing, and the blue
form was filled out incorrectly. "I wonder how on earth that
idiot let this happen," she had said, mostly to herself.

Pilger broke in to ask for the name of the "idiot" in
question.

Her name was Karen, and she had been working at reception the previous night. "It's because of her that we're in
this mess."

George had already had enough of Jarkowiszski's drama-
queen narrative. Since she had not been present when the
events occurred, he asked her for the names and phone
numbers of all staff on duty at the time of the crime and
took his leave.

He called Nathalie from his car and asked her to request
all the people named to drop by the precinct on their way
to work.

By the end of the day he had interviewed them all and
knew that late on Sunday night a fake doctor wearing a coat
stolen from a genuine doctor (a most unpleasant one, apparently) had appeared at the hospital with an ambulance
driver and fake transfer papers. The two accomplices had,
with no difficulty whatever, kidnapped the body of deep-
coma patient Lauren Kline. But last-minute testimony from
an intern caused Pilger to amend his report. The fake doctor
might in fact have been a genuine doctor: apparently, in
an unexpected emergency, the intern had appealed to the
suspect for help, and he had taken charge of the situation.

According to the nurse who had also been present, the deftness with which the stranger had put in a central line had led her to believe that he was a surgeon, or at the very least that he worked as an EMS operative. Pilger asked whether an ordinary nurse could have performed the task. He was told that, yes, nurses were trained for that kind of procedure, but the choices the stranger had made, his instructions to the intern, and his dexterity would lead one to believe he was a physician.

*N*athalie was getting ready to go home when Pilger returned to the office. "So, what have you got on this?" she asked.

"Something that doesn't jibe. A doctor who kidnapped a woman in a coma from the hospital. A professional job, no way of identifying the ambulance he used, forged documents."

"What do you think?"

"I don't know. Maybe organ trafficking. They lift the body, take it to a secret lab, operate, remove what interests them—liver, kidneys, heart, lungs—and sell it to clinics that are short on cash and scruples."

He asked Nathalie if she could get him a list of all the private clinics with operating facilities, particularly those in financial difficulty.

"Listen, hon, it's six o'clock and I'd like to get home. It can wait till tomorrow, can't it? These clinics aren't going to file for Chapter Eleven tonight."

"See how fickle you are? This morning you were all ready to take me to the prom, and now you're turning down an invitation to a night on the town. I need you, Nathalie. Give me a hand, will you?"

"God, George, what a manipulator you are. Anyway, in the mornings you don't sound anything like this."

"Maybe, but right now it's the evening. Are you going to help me? Take Granny's pullover off and come to Uncle George's rescue."

"Gee. When you put it that way, how can I refuse? Have a good evening, George!"

"Nathalie?"

"Yes, George?"

"You're beautiful!"

"George, my heart is not up for grabs."

"I wasn't aiming so high, baby."

"Did you make that up?"

"No."

"Didn't think so."

"Okay then, go home, I'll manage."

Nathalie walked to the door, then turned. "Sure you'll be okay?"

"Yeah, yeah, go feed your cat."

"I'm allergic to cats."

"So stay and help me."

"'Night, George." She ran down the stairs, sliding her hand along the rail.

The night shift got down to work. Pilger returned to his screen and connected to the mainframe. He tapped out the word *clinic* on his keyboard and lit a cigarette as he waited for the search. A few minutes later his printer began to chatter as it spewed out some sixty pages. Pilger grumpily retrieved the pile and took it to his desk. "No more than that? And to find out which clinics are feeling the heat, all I have to do is contact a couple of hundred local banks and ask for a list of private clinics seeking bank loans in the last ten months."

He had been talking out loud, and from the gloom of the front door he heard Nathalie's voice asking him, "Why the last ten months?"

"Cop's intuition," he said as he swung around in his chair, a big grin brightening his face. "Why did you come back?"

"Female intuition."

"Well, it's real nice of you."

"All depends on where you take me for dinner. Any leads?"

He did have one idea, but it just looked too basic. He wanted Nathalie to call headquarters and ask whether they'd received any reports about ambulances missing on Sunday night. "You never know, we might get lucky," he said.

Nathalie picked up the phone. The duty cop at the other end of the line carried out a search on his terminal, but told her there had been no such report. Nathalie asked him to broaden his search beyond the city center, but again the search drew a blank. The duty officer was sorry, but no emergency vehicle had been ticketed or reported missing on Sunday night. She asked him to get back to her if any new information came up, then turned again to Pilger.

"Sorry, nothing."

"In that case let's go for dinner. The banks won't tell us anything at this time of night."

They went to Perry's and sat by the window overlooking Union Street. George listened absentmindedly to Nathalie.

"How long have we known each other, George?"

"Long enough for you to still tolerate me, not long enough for you to be fed up." But Pilger was in no mood for banter.

"This clinic thing doesn't work. I keep looking for the motive. Where's the jackpot?"

"Maybe the mother has some ideas. When are you seeing her?"

"Tomorrow."

"Or maybe she's the one, maybe she's had enough of going to the hospital every day."

"No, not a mother, much too risky."

"I mean that maybe she wanted to end it all. Having to see your child in that state day after day. Maybe she just wanted to have it be over, you know?"

"Can you imagine a mother dreaming up a scenario like that to kill her own daughter?"

"No, you're right, it's just too twisted."

"Without a motive we'll get nowhere on this."

"There's always your clinic idea."

"I think that's a dead end, too. It doesn't feel right."

"Why? And if it isn't solid, why did you ask me to stay and work with you tonight?"

"I wanted you to stay and have dinner with me tonight. When you think about it, stealing a body for its organs is just too high-visibility. They couldn't hope to do it again. Every hospital in the county would be on the alert, and I don't believe the price of one body is worth the risk. How much would I get for a kidney?"

"Two kidneys, a liver, and a heart: I'd think around a hundred and fifty thousand dollars, maybe."

"A lot more expensive than a T-bone!"

"You're disgusting."

"And you see, that route doesn't lead anywhere either. A hundred and fifty grand would be no use to a clinic staring at hard times. This thing isn't about money."

"Maybe it's about availability," Nathalie suggested.

"What do you mean?"

She explained: for some people, the availability of a compatible organ was a question of life or death. People died because they failed to receive the kidney or liver they needed in time. Someone with enough money could have masterminded the kidnapping of a person in an irreversible coma in order to save one of his children's lives, or his own.

Pilger found her theory credible but complicated. If they followed up on it, that would add substantially to the range of suspects. They would no longer necessarily be stalking a professional criminal. Many people might be tempted to do away with someone already acknowledged to be brain-dead, if it meant saving their own life or the life of their child. You might almost feel absolved of the notion of murder, if the victim was brain-dead anyway and you were saving someone else's life.

"You think we'll have to do the rounds of all the clinics to identify a financially well-off patient who's waiting for an organ donor?" she asked.

"I hope not, because it would be ball-breaking, and in tricky terrain."

Nathalie's cell phone rang. Apologizing to Pilger, she picked up, listened carefully, scribbled some notes, and thanked her caller several times.

"Who was that?"

"The duty guy at headquarters, the one I called a while ago."

"And?"

The officer had decided to send out a message to all night patrols, to make sure that no one had noted suspicious activity involving an ambulance, whether or not a report had been filed.

"And?"

"Well, it was a good decision, because a patrol did intercept and tail an ambulance that was driving around and around the Green, Webster, Union, and Fillmore block last night."

"Smells good. What did they say?"

"They stopped the ambulance driver and he told them the ambulance was going into retirement after ten years' faithful service. They figured the driver had gotten attached to his vehicle and was putting off the moment he'd have to turn it in."

"What was the model?"

"A '71 Ford."

Pilger made a swift mental calculation. If the Ford heading for the junkyard last night after ten years' service was really a '71, it must have been kept under wraps for sixteen years before being put to work. The driver had given the officers a line. At last they were on to something.

"It gets better," Nathalie said.

"How?"

"When the driver finally took the ambulance to the garage, they tailed him. They have the address."

"You know, Nathalie, it's a good thing we're not romantically involved."

"Why do you say that now?"

"Because with the trouble this guy just took to get you this information, I'd have proof that you're cheating on me."

"You're an idiot, George. Do you want to go over there right away?"

"No. Tomorrow morning will do. The garage is probably closed now, and there's nothing I can do without a warrant. I'd just as soon go there without attracting attention. It's not the ambulance I'm after, but the guys who used it. Better to go there as a tourist; that way, we won't send the rabbits scuttling for their burrows."

Pilger paid the check and they headed outside. "Mind if we take a walk?" he asked. The ambulance had been spotted at an intersection close to the restaurant where they had eaten, and George wanted to scan the area, at least.

"Know what would really make me happy?" said Nathalie.

"No, but you're about to tell me."

"If you'd come sleep at my place. I don't feel like sleeping alone tonight."

"Do you have a toothbrush?"

"Yes. Yours."

"I like teasing you, you're the only one who's any fun. Let's go—I wanted to stay with you tonight, too. It's been a long time."

"It was just last Thursday."

"Like I said."

By the time they switched off the lights an hour and a half later, George told Nathalie he was convinced he would solve the case.

"Then you will," Nathalie assured him. "As we know, when you're convinced of something, you're wrong only fifty percent of the time."

*T*uesday was a productive day. Pilger had a long, rather painful meeting with Mrs. Kline and absolved her of all suspicion once he learned of the decision she and the doctors had come to the previous week. The mother was cooperative, she was obviously shattered, and Pilger by now had developed a sixth sense that could detect when people were faking emotional pain.

At the garage, he had tracked down the offending vehicle. He was surprised when he first entered the establishment, which contained nothing but ambulances in various stages of repair. It was not the kind of place one could "drop by" unnoticed. Forty mechanics and about a dozen clerical staff worked there: in all, more than fifty potential suspects. The owner listened doubtfully to the inspector and wondered what had possessed the perpetrators to return the vehicle instead of getting rid of it. Pilger told him that a theft would have attracted the attention of the police, who would have made the necessary connections. One of the owner's employees was probably involved, Pilger suggested, and was hoping that the "loan" would go unnoticed.

Now all they had to do was find which of the employees was involved. None, the owner said—the lock showed no sign of being forced, and no one but him had a key to the night alarm. Pilger questioned the shop foreman about what might have led the "borrowers" to pick this particular make and was told that a '71 Ford was the only one that could be driven like a regular car. That was one more reason for Pilger to believe that one of the employees was involved. Asked whether it was possible for someone to take the key and make a double, the owner replied, "It's conceivable, when we close the main entrance at noon."

So all of them were suspects. Pilger asked the owner for the employee records. On top of the pile he put the folders of all those who had left in the past two years. When he returned to his office at around two, Nathalie was still not back from her lunch break. He buried himself in a detailed analysis of the fifty-seven brown folders he had put on his desk. Nathalie arrived around three, sporting a new hairstyle and braced for sarcastic comments.

"Not a word, George, you'll only say something stupid," she said before she had even put down her purse.

He looked up from his papers and smiled. Before he could say a thing, she came over to him and laid her finger on his lips to silence any commentary. "Something's come up that's a lot more interesting than my hairdo, but I'll tell you only if you promise to hold the jokes, okay?"

He mimicked the expression of someone with a gag over his mouth and grunted a monosyllabic groan of agreement. Nathalie withdrew her finger.

"The girl's mother phoned. She remembered something that might be important to your inquiry, and she wants you to call her. She's at home, waiting to hear from you."

"But I love your hairdo, it really suits you," he protested as soon as she was finished.

Nathalie smiled and returned to her desk.

Over the phone, Mrs. Kline told Pilger of her strange conversation with the young man she had met by accident in the Marina a few days ago—the young man who had lectured her so earnestly about the sanctity of life.

She repeated every detail of the encounter. He had told her he was an architect; he claimed to have met Lauren in the emergency room after gashing his hand with a box cutter. He also claimed to have lunched with her daughter often since then, but although the dog did seem to recognize him, Mrs. Kline did not believe he was really a friend of her daughter's. Lauren had never mentioned him, though he had said he had known her for two years.

That last detail should certainly help his investigation, she added.

"Well, well," murmured the policeman. "So you want me to look for an architect who cut his hand two years ago, who claims that your daughter stitched him up, and you believe we should suspect him because he talked to you about euthanasia in a chance meeting?"

"Doesn't it strike you as a credible lead?"

"Not really, but I'll follow it up all the same."

"So what do you think?" Nathalie asked when he had hung up the phone.

"I think your hair looked nicer before."

"Okay, okay, so it was a false alarm!"

Pilger returned to his folders, but not one of them yielded a clue. Thoroughly exasperated, he picked up the phone, wedged it between his ear and shoulder, and dialed the number for the hospital switchboard. The operator picked up at the ninth ring.

"It took you so long to answer, I could have died!"

"In that case, call the morgue," the operator shot back.

Pilger identified himself and asked whether the hospital computers could conduct a search through emergency admissions by patient's profession and type of injury. "It depends on the time frame you're interested in," the woman told him. But medical confidentiality prohibited her from giving out such information, she added, particularly by phone. He hung up on her, grabbed his raincoat, and walked to his car. Impatient, he crossed town, his flashing red light attached to the roof, siren howling. Scarcely ten minutes later, he was at Memorial Hospital. He planted himself in front of the receptionist's desk.

"You asked me to find a woman in a coma who was

removed from this place on Sunday night, and now you tell me you can't give me information necessary to my investigation. Now, either you cooperate and can the crap about medical confidentiality or I drop the whole thing."

Head Nurse Jarkowiszski appeared from a nearby doorway. "How may I help you?"

"I need to know if your computers can trace an architect who was apparently injured and treated here by your missing patient."

"What is the time frame?"

"Let's say two years."

"We'll search through admissions for an architect. It will take a few minutes."

"I'll wait."

Jarkowiszski returned ten minutes later. No architect had been treated for the injury in question in the past two years.

"You're sure?"

She was quite sure. Filling in the "profession" box was mandatory for insurance purposes, and to maintain the statistics on work-related injuries. Pilger thanked her. Well, that was one dead end followed through on, he thought to himself as he drove back to the precinct. But the whole business about the architect and his conversation with the mother was beginning to gnaw at him. When a clue bothered him this way, it could monopolize his full attention, making him forget all his other possible leads. He took out his cell phone and called Nathalie.

"Find out if there's an architect living in the area where they spotted the ambulance."

"Union, Fillmore, and Green?"

"And Webster, but extend the search to cover that whole section of Pacific Heights."

"I'll call you back."

When he got back to the office, Nathalie told him three architecture firms and one architect's residence were in the specified area. Only the residence was in the immediate area. One of the firms was located on the next street, and the other was two streets away. Pilger contacted the three firms to take a tally of the employees. There were twenty-seven in all. By 6:30 PM he had over eighty suspects. One of those people could be waiting for an organ for himself or someone close to him.

He thought a moment, then turned to Nathalie.

"Do we have any extra rookies hanging around?"

"We never have anyone to spare. If we did, I'd get home at a decent hour and wouldn't have to live like an old maid."

"Don't be so hard on yourself, sweetheart. Why don't you find me someone, and have him stake out the house belonging to the guy who lives in our area. See if he can't get me a photo when the guy gets home from work."

*N*ext morning, Pilger learned that the rookie had drawn a blank. The man had not come home.

"Bingo," Pilger said to the young detective. "By tonight I want you to know everything about this man: how old he is, is he a homo, on drugs, was he in the service, where'd he go to school, where does he work, does he have a dog, a cat, a parrot. You can call the army, the FBI, I don't care, but we have to know everything."

"*I'm* a homo, Inspector," the rookie retorted sarcastically. "I'll try not to let that get in my way."

The inspector spent the rest of the day morosely trying to make sense of the leads he was following. He found

nothing to cheer him. While the ambulance had been identified, thanks to a stroke of fortune, none of the body-shop
employee records pointed to a possible suspect, which meant
that hours of interviews awaited him. More than sixty archi-
tects would have to be questioned too, since they worked or
lived near the block that the ambulance had circled on the
night of the kidnapping.

One of them might possibly be a suspect because he had
stroked the victim's mother's dog and stated his opposition
to euthanasia one morning. It didn't exactly constitute a
solid motive for kidnapping, Pilger had to admit. A real "shit
inquiry," as he thoughtfully put it.

The sun that rose over Carmel that Wednesday morning
shone through the faintest of mists. Lauren woke early. She
had left the bedroom in order not to wake Arthur, and was
fuming at her inability to make breakfast for him. Still, she
was happy that despite this incomprehensibly tangled mess,
he had, somehow, been able to touch her, to feel her, and
even more amazingly, to love her as if she were a woman in
full possession of her body. They had already been through
an entire spectrum of impossible things, things she would
never understand—things she had decided to stop trying to
comprehend.

She recalled what her father had told her one day: "Nothing's impossible. The mind's limitations just tell us that certain things are beyond our understanding. Often we have to
solve a whole bunch of equations before we can accept new
ideas. It's a question of time and of the limits of our brains.
Performing a cardiac bypass, getting a three-hundred-and-
fifty-ton aircraft to fly, walking on the moon—it all took

work, but most of all it took imagination. So when people tell you it's impossible to transplant a brain, or fly at the speed of light, or clone a human being, you just settle back and imagine that everything is possible—it will just take time to figure out how."

Everything Lauren was living and experiencing was illogical, beyond explanation, in violation of every scientific truth she had ever absorbed; and yet, it *was*. She had made love with a man and felt emotions and sensations she had never known even when she was well—even when her body and spirit were one. What was most important to her, as she watched the fireball rise slowly above the horizon, was that it should continue.

*A*rthur woke shortly after she left. He searched for her throughout the house, then put on a bathrobe and strolled out back. He spotted her sitting on the rocks. His arms were around her before she even realized he was there.

"Quite a sight," he whispered in her ear.

"You know, I was thinking, since we can't plan for the future we should close the suitcase and live in the present. Would you like coffee?"

"Coffee is vitally necessary. And then I'll take you to watch the sea lions swimming over by the headland."

"Real sea lions?"

"And seals, and pelicans, and . . ." He cupped her face in his hands and kissed her.

*O*n Thursday morning, Pilger's rookie delivered the file he'd compiled, with some ceremony.

"What did you come up with?" Pilger asked before the young detective had even opened it.

"Good news and bad news."

In a show of impatience verging on exasperation, Pilger tapped the knot of his necktie a couple of times: "One, two; one, two. Testing, testing. All systems go, kid, the mike's working, it's all yours!"

The rookie read out his notes. There was nothing unusual about his architect. He could not have been more normal: he did not take drugs; was highly regarded in his profession; had no police record. He had studied in California and lived for some time in Europe before returning to settle in his native city. He belonged to no political party, was a member of no sect, was an activist in no cause. He paid his taxes and his parking tickets and had never been stopped for driving under the influence or over the speed limit. "In other words, a pretty boring guy."

"And what's the good news?"

"He's not even a homo."

"Christ, I don't have anything against homos—cut it out, will you? What else have you got in that report?"

"His last address, his photo—it's kind of old, I got it from Motor Vehicles, taken four years ago, his license comes up for renewal at the end of this year—an article he wrote for *Architectural Digest,* copies of his degrees, and a list of his bank holdings and real estate."

"How did you get your hands on that?"

"My boyfriend works for the IRS. This architect of yours is an orphan; his folks left him a house in Carmel."

"Think he's vacationing there?"

"Yes, he's there now. In fact, that house of his is actually the 'good news' I mentioned."

"What do you mean?"

"Well, there's no phone there, which struck me as odd for such an isolated place. It was disconnected more than five years ago and has never been hooked up since. On the other hand, he had the power and water turned back on just last Friday. In other words, he went back to that house last weekend for the first time in a long while. Of course, that's no crime."

"But you're right: that last bit of news could ring the jackpot. You've done a great job. With a mind as twisted as yours, you'll make a fine cop."

"Coming from you, I guess I should take that as a compliment."

"You sure can!" called Nathalie.

"Now," Pilger instructed, "take that photo to Mrs. Kline—I'll give you the address—and ask her if he's the guy from the Marina who doesn't like euthanasia. If she fingers him, we're on to something solid."

The rookie left the precinct and George Pilger buried himself in Arthur's file. An hour later the rookie informed him that Mrs. Kline had identified the man in the photo. But the real break came just as Pilger was taking Nathalie out to lunch. It was sitting right under his nose, but he had failed to make the connection. The kidnap victim's former address was the same as the young architect's. With that many leads, he had to be involved in this business.

*E*verything's coming together, you should be happy. So why are you pulling that face?" asked Nathalie as she sipped her diet Coke.

"Because I still don't see what he could be after. This guy

doesn't have the profile of a nut. You don't go swipe a comatose body from the hospital just to give your friends a
laugh. You have to have a real reason. Besides, according to
the folks at the hospital, not just anyone can place a central
bridge."

"It's a central line. Not a bridge. Was he her boyfriend?"

Mrs. Kline had sworn he was not. She was almost certain
they had never met.

"Some connection through the apartment?" asked
Nathalie.

Not that either, the inspector said. Arthur had rented the
place, and according to the real estate people, he had
landed there by pure chance. He had been on the point of
signing for another apartment on Filmore, but at the last
moment a zealous Realtor had insisted on showing him this
one.

"So there's no premeditation in the choice of address."

"No, it's a genuine coincidence."

"Then is he really the guy?"

"I can't say that," Pilger answered thoughtfully. Taken
separately, none of the clues they'd uncovered implicated
Arthur. But the way the separate pieces of the puzzle fit together was disturbing. Even so, without a motive Pilger could
do nothing. "You can't charge a guy because for the last few
months he's been renting the apartment of a woman who
was kidnapped this week. At least, I'll have trouble finding
a DA who'll go along with it."

Nathalie suggested that Pilger call him in for questioning,
grill him a little.

The old cop cackled. "I can just hear it: 'Sir, you have been
renting the apartment of a young woman in a coma who
was kidnapped on Sunday night. You had the water and

electricity turned back on in your weekend house on the Friday preceding the crime. Why?' And he looks right back and says he isn't absolutely sure he understands the point of my question. All I could do then would be to tell him right out that he's my only lead, and it would make my day if he really had pulled off this kidnapping."

"So take two days off and tail him."

"Without a warrant, anything I bring back will be null and void."

"Not if you bring the body back, and it's still alive."

"You believe it's him?"

"I believe in your flair for this stuff. I believe in our leads, and I believe that when you're wearing that expression, it means you know you have the guy but you just don't yet know how to nail him. George, the most important thing is to find the girl. She may be in a coma, but she's still a hostage. So why don't you pay the check and get the heck out of here?"

Suddenly energized, Pilger rose, kissed Nathalie's forehead, dropped a couple of bills on the table, and hurried out to the street. During the drive to Carmel, Pilger analyzed, again and again, the architect's possible motives. And he planned how he would approach his prey without arousing suspicion.

Chapter
THIRTEEN

*L*ittle by little, the house came back to life again. Like small children carefully coloring in a line drawing, Arthur and Lauren went from room to room, pulled back shutters, stripped dustcovers from the furniture, dusted, polished, and opened closet after closet. And little by little, Arthur's memories of the house glided into the present tense. Life was taking hold of the place. That Thursday morning the sky was overcast. Down at the foot of the garden the ocean hurled itself at the rocks as if they were blocking its way. When evening came, Lauren settled down on the porch and gazed at the drama unfolding below. The water had turned gray, with seaweed and matted pine needles bobbing on its surface. The sky darkened to purple, then black. Lauren loved watching nature fly into a rage.

Arthur sat down on the cushioned window seat near Lauren and looked over at her.

"You realize that's the ninth time you've changed clothes since breakfast."

"I know. It's because of the catalogue you brought in. I can't make my mind up, everything looks great."

"Any woman would dream of shopping your way."

"You haven't even seen the next section!"

"What's the next section?"

"Lingerie."

Arthur was mesmerized for some time by the most alluring display a man could dream of. Later, tenderly wrapped around each other, their bodies and minds at rest, they lay close together in the dark, watching the ocean. At last they fell asleep, lulled by the rhythm of the ebbing tide.

*P*ilger arrived at nightfall and checked in at the Carmel Valley Inn. The reception clerk gave him the keys to a small room facing the sea. He had barely started to unpack when the first flashes of lightning slashed across the sky. He lived no more than three hours' ride away, but he had never taken the time to come and visit this spectacular vista. He felt an urge to call Nathalie: someone else should be sharing this with him. He lifted the phone, took a breath, and then softly replaced it. Nah.

He ordered room service, settled down to watch a movie, and was overcome by sleep well before ten.

*T*he next morning, the sun rose so bright that it terrified the clouds out of the sky. Dew shone on the grass. Arthur woke, still lying out on the porch. Lauren was deep in slumber—sleep was still new for her. At the top of the sloping garden, hidden behind the bushes near the gateway, George Pilger was watching through the pair of long-range binoculars he had been given to commemorate his first twenty years of service. At around eleven AM he spotted Arthur walking up the grass in his direction. The suspect veered right at the rose garden and opened the door of the garage.

*W*hen he entered the garage, Arthur found himself facing a tarpaulin thick with dust. He raised it and saw the long lines of a 1961 Ford station wagon. It was a woody—the kind the surfers used to ride in—and in collectible condition, too. Smiling as he remembered Anthony's fastidiousness, Arthur walked around the car and opened the left rear door. The smell of old leather filled his nostrils. He could almost hear the motor purr. He sat in the passenger seat, rolled down the window, poked his head out, and felt his hair blown back by the wind of memories. He stuck out his arm, bending his elbow, and his hand became an airplane. He tilted it to modify the takeoff, felt it swoop up to the garage roof and nosedive back down.

When he opened his eyes again, he saw a small note attached to the steering wheel:

Arthur, if you feel like starting her up, you'll find a battery charger on the shelf to the right. Step on the gas pedal twice before you switch the engine on. That will start the gas flowing. Don't be surprised if it starts up right away: that's normal, for a 1961 Ford. To inflate the tires, the pump's in its box, under the charger.

Love, Anthony.

He got out of the car, shut the door, and walked to the utility shelf in the corner. Then he caught sight of the rowboat. Beneath its wooden seat was a long-decayed baited hook—one of his, the green thread wound around the small cork spool with a rusted hook at the end of it. He marveled at Anthony's sentimentality as he located the charger in the opposite corner, opened the old Ford's hood, connected the cables, and began charging the battery. As he left the garage, he rolled the doors back and left them wide open.

*G*eorge took out his notebook and started writing, his eyes trained on the suspect. He watched him set up a table under the arbor, sit down to breakfast, then clear the table. When Arthur sank onto the cushions in the shade of the patio, George took a sandwich break. When Arthur returned to the garage, George followed his movements. He heard the sound of the tire pump and then, much more distinctly, the roar of the V6 engine starting up after a couple of coughs. He watched the car in admiration as it rolled to a stop by the porch. At four-thirty, just as dusk was coming on, he decided to break off his vigil and get back to the village to glean more information about this odd character.

He called Nathalie.

"So," she said, "are you getting somewhere?"

"Nowhere. Nothing abnormal. Well, almost nothing. He's on his own, he busies himself all day long, he cleans up, fixes things, takes lunch and dinner breaks. I've talked to the local merchants. The house belonged to his mother, who died years ago. The caretaker went on living in the house until he died more than five years ago. None of that gets me very far. He has every right to reopen his mother's house whenever he wants to."

"You said 'almost nothing'?" Nathalie prompted.

George admired her. She never missed a trick. "Because he has some strange habits. He talks to himself, he behaves at his meals as though someone were with him. Sometimes he sits looking at the sea with his arm held straight out for ten minutes."

"What else?"

"At one point he looked like he was holding someone and kissing them, but there was nothing there."

"Maybe he was reliving his dreams in some way?"

"There's a whole lot of 'maybes' about this guy."

"Do you still think he's got something to do with it?"

"I don't know, sweetheart. In any case there's something not right about his behavior."

"Not right?"

"He's unbelievably calm for someone who's guilty."

"So you still believe it's him."

"I'll give myself another day, then I'm coming back. Tomorrow I'm going to pay him a visit."

"Be careful!"

He hung up, his face thoughtful.

*A*rthur sat at the piano and ran his fingertips along the keys. Although it was no longer in tune, he had made a start on the "Clair de lune" from Massenet's *Werther,* avoiding a couple of notes that were now truly discordant. It had been Lili's favorite piece. He talked to Lauren as he played. She was sitting in her favorite position on the window seat, one leg lying along the sill, the other folded beneath her, her back against the wall.

"Tomorrow I'll run a few errands in town; there's almost nothing left to eat."

"Arthur, how long do you intend to go on neglecting the rest of your life?"

"Do we really have to talk about this right now?"

"I may remain in this condition for years. Do you realize what you're getting into? What about your work, your responsibilities, your world?"

"What do you mean, my world? I don't have a world. Listen, Lauren, we've been here less than a week and I haven't taken a vacation in two years, so give me a little time."

"You certainly do have a world. We all do. Love isn't enough for two people to make a success of sharing a life—they have to be compatible, they have to meet each other at the right moment. And that isn't really the case with you and me."

"Have I told you lately that I love you?" he asked timidly.

"You've given me proof. That's much better." Lauren didn't believe it could be just chance. Why was he the only being on this planet she could talk to, communicate with? Why did they get along this way—why did she feel as though he knew everything about her? She said, suddenly, "Why do you give me so much, when I can give you so little?"

"Because all of a sudden there you were. You exist. And just one moment with you is the whole world to me. Yesterday is gone, tomorrow doesn't yet exist. It's today, it's the present, that counts. So I have only one option—to do everything I can to stop you from dying, and to keep you with me."

But that was the problem, Lauren said. She was frightened of the unknown, of what might lie ahead.

"Tomorrow will be whatever we want it to be," he said, to reassure her. "Tomorrow is a mystery for everyone. It should make us curious and happy, not afraid." He took her head in his hands, kissed her eyelids, and pressed her to him. The night was dark around them.

*A*rthur was cleaning out the trunk of the old Ford the next morning when he noticed a dust trail on the crest of the ridge. Pilger drove recklessly down the track and stopped his car by the porch.

"Good morning, can I help you?"

"I drove here from Monterey. The real-estate guy told me this house was unoccupied, and since I'm looking to buy around here I thought I'd come over and see it. But apparently it's already been sold. I guess I'm too late."

Arthur replied that the house had not been sold, nor was it for sale; it was his mother's house, and he had just opened it up. It was a hot afternoon, and Arthur had been gardening: he was dying for lemonade, and offered some to his unexpected visitor. The old cop declined, saying he did not want to be a nuisance, but Arthur insisted and asked him to take a seat on the porch; he would be back in five minutes. He closed the rear hatch of the station wagon, disappeared into the house, and returned with a tray, two glasses, and a jug of lemons in water.

"It's a beautiful house," said Pilger as he looked around. "There can't be too many more like it around here."

"I don't know. I haven't been back here for years."

"What brought you back all of a sudden?"

"I figured it was time."

"Just like that, no particular reason?"

Arthur was suddenly uneasy. This stranger was asking excessively personal questions, as though he knew something he didn't want to reveal. Arthur felt he was being manipulated. But he failed to make the connection with Lauren, believing that he was dealing with some kind of salesman trying to bond with a potential victim.

"In any case, I have no intention of selling it," Arthur said.

"You're right: you don't sell a family home. It would be sacrilege."

Pilger sensed that Arthur was becoming suspicious; it was time to beat a retreat. He announced that he would be heading back to the village "to look for another house." He thanked Arthur warmly for his hospitality, and both men rose. Pilger got into his car, turned the engine on, and drove off with a wave.

Lauren appeared on the porch. "What did he want?"

"To buy this house, or so he said."

"I don't like it."

"Neither do I, but I'm not sure why."

"Do you think he's a cop?"

"No, I think we're paranoid. I don't see how anyone could have tracked us down. I think he was some kind of business promoter, or a Realtor checking out the territory. Don't worry. Now, I have those errands to run. Are you staying or coming with me?"

"I'm coming."

. . .

*T*wenty minutes after Arthur pulled out in the Ford, Pilger came back down the garden path, this time on foot. Reaching the house, he checked the front door and found it was locked, then made a tour of the ground-floor windows. None of them was open, but only one set of storm shutters was closed. Just one room was closed up: it was enough for the old cop to draw conclusions. He did not linger on the premises but returned quickly to his car. Picking up his cell phone, he called Nathalie.

It was a productive conversation. Pilger told her he still lacked proof and clues, but he knew instinctively that Arthur was guilty. Nathalie didn't doubt his nose for a suspect, but Pilger didn't have the warrant he would need in order to lean on the guy, especially with no motive. Finding a motive would be the key to solving this mystery, and he knew it. It had to be substantial for an apparently balanced individual, in no particular financial need, to take such a big risk. But Pilger could not yet see his way to solving this thing. He had considered all the classic motives, and none of them held water. Now he decided to bluff. He would bombard Arthur with false assertions on the off chance of getting at the truth, surprising him into some kind of reaction that might confirm or invalidate Pilger's suspicions. He started the car, drove onto the property, and parked in front of the porch.

Arthur and Lauren returned an hour later and, as Arthur stepped from the Ford, he stared hard at Pilger. The cop came over to meet him.

"I have two things to tell you," said Arthur. "First, the house is not and will not be for sale. And second, this is private property."

"I know, and I couldn't care less if it's for sale or not. Time I introduced myself." Pilger pulled out his badge and thrust it in Arthur's face as he said, "I need to talk to you."

"I believe that's what you're doing."

"May I come in?"

"No, not without a warrant."

"You're making a mistake, playing it this way."

"You made the mistake, lying to me. I welcomed you and gave you something to drink."

"Can we at least sit on the porch?"

"We can. Go ahead."

The two of them sat on the swing seat. Lauren, standing by the steps, was terrified. Arthur glanced over and winked, to let her know everything was under control.

Pilger launched right into his suspicions. "Tell me what your motive is, that's where I'm stuck."

"My motive for what?"

"I'm going to be very frank with you. I know it's you."

"At the risk of seeming a little bit simple, yes, it's true, it's me. I've been me ever since I was born, never any problems with schizophrenia. What on earth are you talking about?"

He was talking, Pilger said, about the body of Lauren Kline. He accused Arthur of stealing it, with the help of an accomplice and an old ambulance, from San Francisco Memorial Hospital last Sunday night. Pilger told him he had tracked the ambulance to a repair shop. He claimed he was convinced that the body was here in this house, and more precisely in the only room whose shutters were closed. "What I don't understand is why. That's what's bugging me." He was close to retirement and didn't want to end his career with an unsolved case. "Frankly, I don't give a damn about putting you behind bars. I've done that all my life, slinging folks into the can so they can come out again a few years later and start over. The most you'd get for this job is five years, so I don't care, but I do want to understand why."

Arthur pretended not to grasp a word of what the policeman was saying. "What's all this about a body and an ambulance?"

"I'm going to waste as little of your time as possible. Would you agree to let me see that room with the closed shutters without a search warrant?"

"No!"

"Why not, if you have nothing to hide?"

"Because the room you're talking about was my mother's, and ever since her death it's been locked. It's the one room that I'm just not ready to open, which is why the shutters are closed. It's been shut up for more than twenty years, and I'm going to cross the threshold only when I'm alone and when I'm ready. I'm certainly not going to do it for some crazy cop who thinks I'm a criminal." Arthur rose. "I hope I've made myself clear."

"Fair enough. Guess I'll be running along, then."

"Yes, please do."

Pilger rose and walked to his car. As he opened the door, he turned and looked Arthur straight in the eye, hesitated a moment, then decided to see his bluff through.

"If you want to visit that room in the strictest privacy, which I understand, you'd better do it tonight. Because I don't give up. I'll be back tomorrow with a warrant, and it'll be too late then for you to do it alone. Of course, you can decide to move the body during the night, but I'm better at the cat-and-mouse stuff than you. I've been at it thirty years, and I'd make your life a nightmare. I'm leaving my card and cell-phone number on the railing here, just in case you have something to tell me."

"You'll never get a warrant!"

"You do your thing, I'll do mine. See you."

With a squeal of brakes, Pilger sped away.

Arthur stood rooted to the spot for several minutes, his heart beating a tattoo of terror.

Chapter
FOURTEEN

*Y*ou have to tell him the truth and try to cut a deal with him!" Lauren said.

"I have to hurry and find a new place to hide your body."

"No, you can't! He'll be lurking around here somewhere, watching us, and he'll catch you in the act. Stop it, Arthur, this is your life! You heard him, you're risking five years in prison!"

But Arthur had a hunch that the cop was bluffing. Without evidence, he would never get a warrant. He explained his back-up plan: when night fell, they'd put the body in the rowboat. "We'll row down the coast and hide you in a cave for two or three days." If the cop came by he'd find nothing, excuse himself, and leave for good.

"He'll keep at it, because he's a cop and he's stubborn," she retorted. "You still have a chance of wriggling out of this. If you save him time in his inquiry, if you talk, maybe he'll get you some kind of plea bargain. Do it now, or it will be too late."

"It's your life that's at stake."

"Arthur, be reasonable, you're just postponing the inevitable. It's too late."

"We'll take the rowboat out tonight."

Arthur turned his back on her and returned back to unloading the trunk of the station wagon. For the rest of the day, the atmosphere between them remained tense. They scarcely spoke or even looked at each other. Later that afternoon she came to stand in his path and put her arms around him. He kissed her softly. "I can't let them take you, you understand that, don't you?" She understood, but she could never agree to let him put himself at risk.

He waited for night to fall before leaving the house through the French doors that led to the bottom of the garden. He walked down by the rocks, and noted glumly that the sea was against them. Enormous waves crashed against the shore, making his plan impossible to execute. The rowboat would smash at the first impact. The ocean was wild, and the wind had come up, whipping the waves higher still. He crouched down and put his head in his hands.

Lauren came up noiselessly, put her hand on his shoulder, and kneeled down beside him. "Let's go back in," she said. "You'll catch cold."

"I—"

"Don't say anything. Take it as a sign. We'll spend the night together without tormenting ourselves, you'll find a solution tomorrow, and maybe the weather will have calmed down by then."

Arthur knew, though, that the high winds signaled the

beginning of a storm that would last at least three days. A sea this wild would never calm down in just one night. They ate dinner in the kitchen, then made a fire in the living room, both of them deep in thought. Arthur struggled, and failed, to come up with an alternate plan. The wind was raging now outside the house, and rain was banging down on the windows; the ocean had launched a pitiless attack against the fortress of rocks.

"I used to love it when nature went wild like this," Arthur said bitterly.

"You seem sad, Arthur, and you shouldn't be. We're not leaving each other. You're always telling me not to think about tomorrow. Let's make the most of the time we have now."

"But I can't. I don't know how to live in the moment anymore, without thinking of the future."

"Every moment is forever." Lauren decided to tell him a story—a game, something that would distract him, she said. She told him to imagine he'd won a contest. The prize was that every morning, a bank would open an account in his name containing 86,400 dollars. There were only two rules: "The first rule is that everything you fail to spend is taken from you that night. You can't cheat, you can't switch the unspent money to another account: you can only spend it. But when you wake next morning, and every morning after that, the bank opens a new account for you, always eighty-six thousand, four hundred dollars, for the day. Rule number two is that the bank can break off the game without warning. It can tell you at any time that it's over, that it's closing the account and there won't be another one. Now, what would you do?"

Arthur wasn't sure he understood.

"It's very simple: every morning when you wake up, they give you eighty-six thousand, four hundred dollars, on the sole condition that you spend it in one day. If you don't spend it all by the time you go to bed, you lose whatever you didn't spend. But this game—this windfall—can stop at any moment, understand? So my question is, what would you do if you were handed a prize like that?"

He didn't have to think long to answer. He'd spend every dollar on pleasure and on gifts for the people he loved. He'd find a way to use up every cent offered by this magic bank to bring happiness into his life and the lives of everyone around him. "And even the lives of people I don't know, because I don't think I'd manage to spend eighty-six thousand, four hundred dollars just on me and my friends every day. But what's your point?"

She answered, "We all have that magic bank account: it's time! A big account, filled with fleeting seconds. Every morning when we wake up, our account for the day is credited with eighty-six thousand, four hundred seconds, and when we go to sleep every night, there's no carryover into the next day. What hasn't been lived during the day is lost; yesterday has vanished. Every morning the magic begins again, with a new line of credit of eighty-six thousand, four hundred seconds. And don't forget rule number two: the bank can close our account at any time and without any warning. At any moment, life can end. So what do we do with our daily ration of eighty-six thousand, four hundred seconds? Aren't seconds of life more important than dollars?"

Since her accident, she told him, she had realized afresh each day how few people understood and appreciated the importance of time. "If you want to know what a year of life means, ask a student who just flunked his year-end exams.

Or a month of life: talk to a mother who has just given birth to a premature baby and is waiting for him to be taken out of the incubator before she can hold him safe and sound in her arms. Or a week: interview a man who works in a factory or a mine to feed his family. Or a day: ask two people madly in love, who are waiting to see each other again. Or an hour: talk to someone with claustrophobia who's stuck in a broken-down elevator. Or a second: look at the expression on the face of a man who has just escaped from a car wreck. Or one thousandth of a second: ask the athlete who just won the silver medal at the Olympic Games, and not the gold he trained for all his life. Life is magic, Arthur, and I know what I'm saying, because since my accident I've appreciated the value of every instant. So I beg you, let's make the most of all the seconds that we have left."

Arthur put his arms around her and said softly into her ear, "Each second with you is worth more than any other second."

They spent the rest of the evening in each other's arms, by the fire.

They were woken early next morning, when Arthur's cell phone rang. The storm was still raging. It was Pilger: he asked Arthur to see him, he had something to tell him and wanted to apologize for the way he'd behaved the previous day. Arthur hesitated, not knowing if the man was still trying to manipulate him or if he was sincere. He looked out at the torrential rain, which Pilger surely wouldn't fail to use as a pretext to ask himself into the house. On the spur of the moment—perhaps hoping to start out with the upper hand—Arthur invited the cop to have lunch. Lauren said nothing, just twisted her face into a sad little smile that Arthur didn't see.

*I*nspector Pilger rang the bell two hours later. When Arthur opened the door, a gust of wind roared into the hallway, and it took the two of them to wrestle the door back shut.

"It's a hurricane!" he exclaimed.

"I'm sure you're not here to discuss the weather report."

Lauren followed them into the kitchen. Arthur had set two places and prepared a Caesar salad with grilled chicken and a mushroom omelette, accompanied by a Napa Valley cabernet.

"This is very nice of you. I didn't expect you to go to all this trouble."

"What causes me trouble, Inspector, is that you're bothering the hell out of me with your ridiculous theories."

"If they're as ridiculous as you claim, I won't be bothering you much longer. So, you're an architect?"

"You know I am."

"What kind of architecture?"

"My real love is restoring historic buildings and interiors."

"Which means?"

"Giving new life to old houses, preserving old stones, adapting them to life today."

Pilger had found the way in: he lured his suspect onto a topic that enthralled him. Arthur's passion for his work was contagious. The old inspector fell into his own trap: having set out to arouse Arthur's interest and forge some basis of communication, he was becoming engrossed in the subject himself.

Arthur gave him a crash course on the history of stonework, from ancient architecture through classical times, with a glimpse of modern and contemporary developments thrown in. The old cop was mesmerized; he asked question after question and Arthur answered them all. Their conversation went on for more than an hour. Pilger learned how his own San Francisco had been rebuilt after the great earthquake of 1906; he heard the history of the buildings he saw every day—a whole series of anecdotes that built up a picture of how the cities and streets he lived in came to be.

Cups of coffee followed, one after the other. Lauren listened, taken aback, to the unexpected kinship that was springing up between Arthur and the inspector.

As Arthur finished a story about the construction of the Golden Gate Bridge, Pilger interrupted him. Putting his hand on Arthur's, he said, "Arthur, I need to talk to you, man to man—not as a cop." He put his badge on the table and took a deep breath. He said he needed to understand this case. He was an old cop whose instinct had never let him down. He felt—he knew—that the body of this woman was being hidden in the closed room at the end of the corridor. But he didn't grasp the motive for the kidnapping. Arthur was the kind of guy any man would want his son to be: good-looking, well-educated, interested in life. He had everything going for him. So why would he risk losing everything to steal the body of a woman in a coma?

Arthur stood up. "It's too bad. I thought we were really becoming friends."

"We are, that's the point! That has nothing to do with it—or maybe it has everything to do with it. I'm sure you have genuinely good reasons for what you did, and I'm offering to help you. I'll be completely honest with you. For starters, I can't get a warrant today: I don't have enough evidence. I'll have to go see the judge in San Francisco, negotiate with him, convince him—but rest assured, I'll get it. It might take two or three days, enough time for you to move the body, but I guarantee that if you do that, you'll be ruining your life."

Pilger paused. "Right now, there's still time for me to help you, and I'm willing to do that, provided you talk to me and explain to me why."

Arthur's reply was tinged with sarcasm. "I appreciate your kindness and your generous offer, and I'm really quite surprised that you feel you've learned so much about me, since we've only just met. There's something I don't understand, too. Here you are, a guest in my home, I've welcomed you in, made you a meal, yet you stubbornly persist in accusing me—without any proof—of a crime that is completely absurd."

"You're the one who's stubborn."

"Why do you want to help me if you think I'm guilty? Just to get another case solved?"

The old cop's reply was sincere. In his career, he had known plenty of cases, crimes of all types, with hundreds of absurd motives—sordid crimes. But the perpetrators all had one thing in common: they were criminals, nuts, maniacs, bad people. Arthur didn't seem to be that type. So after spending his whole life putting bad guys behind bars, if Pilger could now help a decent guy, who'd maybe gotten involved in an impossible situation, evade that fate—"I'd feel that at least for once I was working on the right side of the tracks."

"That's very nice of you, and I mean that. I enjoyed our conversation, but the situation you describe doesn't apply to me. I'm not throwing you out, but I have work to do. Perhaps we'll get a chance to talk again."

Pilger acquiesced with a mournful nod. He got up and retrieved his raincoat. Lauren followed them down the hall leading to the front door.

Outside Lili's room, Pilger stopped, his eyes on the door handle.

"Sometimes it's hard to go back into the past. It takes a lot of strength, a lot of courage."

"Yes, I know, that's just what I'm trying to work up."

"I know I'm not mistaken about you, young man. My instinct has never failed me."

Arthur was on the point of asking Pilger to leave when the door handle of his mother's room began to turn, as though someone were moving it from the inside. Then the door opened. Arthur was stupefied. Lauren stood in the doorway, smiling sadly.

"Why did you do that?" he murmured, his voice choked.

"Because I love you."

From where he stood, Pilger at once saw the body on the bed, the IV tubing suspended above. "Thank God, she's alive." He walked over to the bed and knelt beside it.

Lauren put her arms around Arthur and kissed him tenderly on the cheek.

"I couldn't let you ruin the rest of your life for me. I want you to live free, I want you to be happy."

"You are my happiness."

She put a finger on his lips. "No, not like this, not this way."

"Who are you talking to?" asked the inspector.

"To her."

"You're really going to have to explain this, if you want me to help you out."

Arthur looked despairingly at Lauren.

"You have to tell him the whole truth," she urged. "He may believe you and he may not, but stick to the truth."

Arthur turned to Pilger. "Come on, let's go to the living room. I'm going to tell you the whole thing."

The two men sat down on a large sofa and Arthur told the story, starting from the beginning. That first evening, when an unknown woman hiding in his bathroom closet said to him, "What I have to tell you is not easy to understand. It may seem impossible to accept. But if you'll listen to my story—if you're willing to trust me—then maybe in the end you'll believe me. And it's very important that you, in particular, should believe me. For without knowing it, you're the only person in the world who can share my secret." Pilger heard him through to the end without interrupting. When he finished, evening was drawing in. Arthur looked challengingly at his companion.

"You see, Inspector, a story like this just adds another nutcase to your collection!"

"Is she here, is she nearby?"

"She's sitting in the chair across from you, and she's looking at you."

Pilger rubbed the bristles on his chin and nodded. "Of course. Of course."

"What are you going to do now?" asked Arthur.

Pilger didn't speak for a while, then he sighed and softly said, "I'm going to believe you." He paused a moment to let Arthur take that in. "And if you want to know why, the answer is simple. Because to make up such a story and take the risks you've taken, you would have had to have lost your mind completely. And the man who talked to me about the history of the city I have served for thirty years was definitely not crazy. Your story has to be true for you to do what you did. I don't believe much in God, but I do believe in the human spirit. Anyway, I'm about to retire, and crazy though it may be, I want to believe you."

"So what are you going to do?"

"Can I take her back to the hospital in my car without causing her any harm?"

"Yes, if you're careful," said Arthur, his voice full of distress.

"In that case, I'll keep my end of the bargain: I'll get you out of this mess."

"But I don't want to be separated from her, I don't want them to let her die!"

"That's a whole different battle, my friend. I can't do everything."

Pilger would be taking a big risk just returning the body. He'd have the rest of the night and a drive of more than a hundred miles to come up with a good explanation for how he'd found the victim without identifying the kidnapper. Since she was alive and had suffered no harm, he believed he could arrange to have Lauren's case classified as solved. There was nothing much else he could do, "but that's already a lot, wouldn't you say?"

"Yes," Arthur said. "Thank you."

"I'm going to leave you two alone for the night. I'll be back tomorrow around eight. Make sure she's ready to be moved."

"Why are you doing this?"

"I already told you, because I like you and I respect you. I'll never know if your story is true or if you dreamed it. In any case, from your point of view, you acted in her best interests. A man might almost be persuaded that you were protecting her. I don't care why you did it. Courage is about doing what you think is best when the time comes to act, without considering the consequences." Pilger rose. "Well, enough talk. Make the most of the time you have left."

The policeman got up, and Arthur and Lauren followed him. A violent gust of wind greeted them as they opened the front door.

"See you tomorrow," Pilger said.

"See you tomorrow," Arthur replied.

The old cop drove off into the storm.

*A*rthur couldn't sleep. At first light he went to Lili's study. He got Lauren's body ready for the journey, then went back up to his bedroom to pack his things. He walked through the house, closed all the shutters, turned off the gas and electricity. He and Lauren had spent the night talking, and they had agreed: they would return to their apartment in San Francisco. Lauren couldn't stay far from her body for long without fatigue. When Pilger came for the body, they would follow him back to the city.

The inspector arrived at the appointed hour. Within fifteen minutes, Lauren's body was wrapped in blankets and propped in the backseat of the policeman's car. By nine, the house was closed up and the two cars were on the road. By noon, Pilger had arrived at the hospital; at around the same time, Arthur and Lauren pulled up at the Green Street apartment.

Chapter
FIFTEEN

*P*ilger kept his promise. He deposited his inert passenger in the emergency room of San Francisco Memorial Hospital at 11:17 that morning. Less than an hour later, Lauren's body was back in Room 505. The inspector returned to the precinct and went straight to his chief's office. Nobody ever learned what was said between the two men, but the conversation lasted two hours, and when Pilger left the room he carried a fat folder under his arm. He walked over to Nathalie and dropped the folder on her desk. Looking her straight in the eye, he told her to stamp it CASE CLOSED and file it away.

Arthur and Lauren unloaded their stuff into the apartment. They spent the afternoon in the Marina, walking by the ocean. Perhaps there was hope: Lauren's mother might reverse her decision to let the hospital unplug Lauren. They ate dinner at Prego and returned home around ten PM to watch a movie on television.

Their life together seemed to assume a normal course— so much so, that with each passing day, they were increasingly able to forget their predicament.

From time to time Arthur dropped in at his office to sign papers. He and Lauren spent the rest of their days together, going to movies, taking long walks along the pathways of Golden Gate Park. They spent one weekend at Tiburon, in a house a friend sometimes lent to Arthur when he was out of the country. One weekend they went sailing in the bay, hopping from cove to cove.

They went to performances in the city—ballet, concerts, theater. Time passed the way it does during a lazy vacation, when you go wherever your whim takes you. They lived in the moment, without projecting into the future: just living what was happening now. Remembering Lauren's game, they called it "seconds theory." Passersby assumed that Arthur was crazy when they saw him walking with one arm outstretched or talking to himself. The waiters in the restaurants they frequented were accustomed to this man sitting alone at the table who suddenly leaned over and mimed taking a hand and kissing it, or talked softly to someone who was invisible to everyone else, or stood back at a doorway to let a nonexistent companion pass through. Some people thought he'd lost his mind; others, that he was a widower living in the shadow of his dead wife. Arthur had stopped noticing them; he was relishing every instant that weaved the fabric of his and Lauren's lives together. They had become lovers, friends, companions for life.

Paul no longer worried so much. He managed to rationalize his friend's behavior as some kind of crisis. Relieved that the kidnapping had had no repercussions, he focused on managing the office, convinced that his friend would one day return to his senses and life would resume its pattern. He was in no hurry. Arthur was like a brother to him. The important thing was for him to get well—or, if he did still have to live in his own world, then at least get better.

$\mathcal{T}$hree months had gone by, and still nothing disturbed their private idyll. One Tuesday night they went to bed after a quiet evening at home. After making love, they shared the last lines of a novel they were reading together. (Arthur had to turn Lauren's pages for her.) They fell asleep late, in each other's arms.

At about six the next morning, Lauren suddenly sat up in bed and called Arthur's name. He woke with a start. She was sitting cross-legged on the bed, her skin pale, almost transparent.

"What's wrong?"

"Hold me, Arthur. Quickly. Please."

He did as she asked and wrapped his arms around her. Before he could ask her again, she put her hand on his unshaven chin and stroked it, fondling it with infinite tenderness. Her eyes filled with tears, and she spoke.

"It's time, my love. They're taking me away. I'm fading."

"No!" He tightened his arms around her.

"God, if you knew how much I don't want to leave. I wish our life together didn't have to stop. We've hardly begun yet."

"Don't go! Fight it! Lauren, please!"

"Don't say anything, just listen, I can tell I don't have much time left. You gave me what I didn't know even existed. I never imagined that love could bring so many simple, good things. Nothing in my life before you was worth a single minute of the time we've spent together. I want you always to remember how much I've loved you. I don't know where I'm going, but if an afterlife exists, I'll be loving you there with all the strength and all the joy with which you've filled my life.

"I have the color of your smile in my eyes," she went on. "Thank you for all the laughter and the tenderness."

Already, Lauren was becoming more and more transparent. Her skin became as clear as water. Even as he held her, he felt his arms begin to close on an encroaching void. He felt her becoming evanescent.

"I can't live without you."

"Share what you have with someone else. Don't waste it."

"Stay, Lauren, please."

"I can't, it's stronger than I am. I'm not in pain, you know, I just have the impression you're getting farther and farther away. Your words are muffled. I can't see you properly anymore. I'm so scared, Arthur. I'm so scared without you. Hold me tighter."

"I'm holding you, can't you feel me?"

"Not really, Arthur. Not anymore."

And so they wept, quietly, together. Now more than ever, they realized what a second of life, a single word, can be worth. They embraced. Then, during a kiss they never ended, she vanished altogether. Arthur's arms met around nothing. He curled up and cried out in pain. His whole body was trembling. His head rocked from side to side. His fists were clenched so tight his nails drew blood from his palms.

The "No!" that he continued to howl like a wounded animal resonated in the room, making the windowpanes shake. He tried to get up but swayed and fell to the ground, his arms still wrapped around his torso. He dragged himself to the window seat, where she had so loved to sit, and sat there, numb and devastated. He barely noticed when, hours later, the sun set over the bay.

*A*rthur plunged into the world of absence. It echoed in his head. It filled his veins and dulled his heart. His grief filled him with rage, doubt, and jealousy—not toward other people, but for the lost moments, the time with Lauren that had been stolen from him. Absence changed him, made his senses sharper and keener. He ached for her, his nose sniffing for her scent, his hand searching to stroke her belly, his eyes searching through tears and finding only memories, his skin searching for her skin, his hand closing on thin air.

He stayed in the apartment for days. He drifted from his desk, where he wrote letters to a ghost, back to his bed, where he would gaze at the ceiling blankly. His telephone had been off the hook and lying on its side for a long time. Arthur didn't care; he no longer expected any calls. Nothing was important.

*A*t the end of one stifling day he emerged for air. It was drizzling. Donning a raincoat, he summoned up the strength to cross the street and stand on the opposite sidewalk.

He stared at the little street, all black and white, like a sketch. His apartment house lay at one end of the block, with a small garden. Only one window still shone with light in the moonless evening: the one in his living room. It had stopped raining. Behind the windowpanes he still sensed Lauren's presence, her graceful movements.

In the shadows of the pavement he felt as though he could see her supple form disappearing around the corner. He thrust his hands into his raincoat pockets, hunched his shoulders, and began to walk after it.

Along the gray and white walls he followed in Lauren's footsteps, careful not to come up too close. At the end of the block, he hesitated a moment, and then, faced with the empty drizzle of the night, and numb with cold, he sat down on the curb. The memory of his mother filled his mind. "Arthur, life is about doubt and about choices," she had told him. "Remember how to choose." The sky grew pale, announcing the dawn of a colorless day.

Arthur hauled himself to his feet, took one last look, and turned away with a guilty sense of having failed. He headed home.

Arthur was lying down on the living-room carpet, watching the birds wheeling in the sky, when someone hammered at the door. He didn't get up.

"Arthur, are you there? I know you're inside! Open the door, for God's sake! Open it!" Paul yelled. "Open up or I'll break it down."

The door shuddered under the impact of Paul's shoulder.

"Shit! That hurt like hell! I think I've broken my collarbone. Open the goddamn door!"

Arthur got up and went to the door, flipped the lock, and returned to the couch. When Paul came in, he gaped at the state of the apartment. Dozens of scraps of paper were strewn across the floor, covered in scribbles. Half-empty food cans littered the kitchen counters. The sink overflowed with dirty dishes.

"So, I guess there's been a war here, and you lost?"

Arthur did not answer.

"So they tortured you, they cut your vocal cords. Boy, do you look like shit. Are you paralyzed, or did you just drink so much you're still out of it?"

Again, Arthur did not answer. Paul could see that he had begun crying. He sat down beside him and put his arm around his shoulder.

"Arthur, what's going on?"

"She's dead, she died ten days ago. She began to disappear, just like that. They killed her. I can't get over it, Paul. I can't."

"I can see that." Paul took Arthur in his arms and held him tight. "Go on, cry, buddy, cry, cry all you want. They say it helps you get over it."

"But that's all I've been doing!"

"Well, keep right on going. Looks as if there's more where that came from."

Paul noticed the phone lying with the receiver off the cradle. He got up and replaced it.

"I've called you two hundred times, but it didn't occur to you to put the phone back on the hook!"

"Screw the phone, Paul!"

"You have to snap out of this, pal. You know, this whole business with the ghost was too much. You took it too far, and now it looks as if it's taking you too far. You dreamed it, Arthur. You had a crazy ride. Now you have to come back to reality. You're screwing up your life. You're not working, you look like a homeless guy on a good night, you're thin as a nail—you look like a refugee. We haven't seen you at the office for weeks. People are wondering about you. You fell in love with a woman in a coma, you made up this whole crazy story, you stole her body, and now you're mourning a ghost. Some shrink in this city is going to be a billionaire. You need help, my friend. I'm not leaving you like this."

Paul was interrupted by the sound of the phone ringing. He picked it up, then handed it to Arthur.

"It's some cop. He's pissed as hell. Says it's urgent."

"I have nothing to say to him."

Paul put his hand over the mouthpiece. "Speak to him or I'll shove the phone down your throat." He pressed the phone to Arthur's ear. Arthur listened, then jumped to his feet. He thanked Pilger for calling, then began searching frantically for his keys.

"Mind telling me what's going on?" Paul asked.

"No time, got to find my keys."

"Are they coming to arrest you?"

"No! Cut the crap and help me find my keys!"

"You must be feeling better if you're mouthing off at me again."

Arthur found his keys, apologized to Paul, told him he had no time to explain but that he would call him that night. Paul was wide-eyed. "I don't know where you're heading, but if you're going to be seen in public, I suggest you change clothes and splash some water on your face."

Arthur hesitated, glanced at his reflection in the living-room mirror, and dashed into the bathroom. He kept his head turned away from the closet. Some places will always be painful. In a few minutes he was washed, shaved, and changed. He raced down the stairs to the garage without even saying good-bye.

. . .

*A*fter driving across the city as fast as he could, Arthur parked at San Francisco Memorial Hospital. Not bothering to lock the car doors, he raced inside. Pilger was waiting for him, sitting in an armchair in the reception area. He got up and took his shoulder, trying to calm him down. Lauren's mother was in the hospital, too. Under the circumstances, Pilger had explained everything to her—well, almost everything. She would be waiting for Arthur outside the elevator, on the fifth floor.

Chapter
SIXTEEN

Mrs. Kline was sitting on a chair by the elevator near the intensive-care ward. As soon as she saw him, she got up. She put her arms around him and kissed him on the cheek.

"I don't know you. We only met that one time down in the Marina. But the dog did recognize you. I don't understand what this is all about—I can't understand all of it—but I do know that I owe you more than I can say. I can never thank you enough."

Then she filled in the details Pilger had omitted on the phone. Lauren had emerged from her coma ten days ago. Nobody knew why, but one morning her electroencephalograph, which had been flat for months, had begun beeping, signaling intense electrical activity. A night nurse had noticed it first. She had called an intern, and within minutes the room had become alive with a swarm of doctors, many of them there merely to gape at the woman who had apparently returned from deep coma.

Lauren had remained unconscious for a few days. Then, gradually, she began to move her hands. Yesterday she had opened her eyes and kept them open for hours, seeming to scrutinize everything around her; she still appeared incapable of speaking or emitting sounds. Several doctors were of the opinion that she would have to be taught to speak again; others felt speech might return spontaneously, like her other faculties. Last night she had answered a question with a slight blink of her eyes. She was weak, and lifting her arm seemed too much for her. The doctors said her muscles had atrophied after her long months in bed; they would grow stronger with physiotherapy. The brain scans looked promising; but only time would tell to what degree she would recover.

Arthur couldn't even listen to the end of this report; he had already burst into the room. The cardiac monitor was emitting a regular and reassuring beep. Lauren was sleeping, with her eyes closed. Her skin was still pale, but her beauty was unchanged. He was overcome by emotion when he saw her. He sat down beside the bed and, taking her hand in his, kissed the curve of her palm. Then he settled into a chair and remained there for hours, watching her.

As night fell she opened her eyes, looked at him intently, and smiled.

"Everything's fine, I'm here," he said softly. "Don't tire yourself. You'll be talking soon."

She frowned, hesitated, gave him another smile, then fell back to sleep.

. . .

*A*rthur returned to the hospital every day. He and Mrs. Kline alternated shifts, so that one of them was always near Lauren. One day he found Mrs. Kline waiting for him as he left the elevator; she announced that Lauren had recovered the power of speech that morning. She had spoken a few words in a hoarse, rasping voice.

Arthur went in and sat down beside her. She was sleeping. He ran his hand over her hair and softly stroked her forehead, whispering, "How I've missed the sound of your voice."

She opened her eyes and placed her hand on his. She looked at him with wondering eyes as she asked, "Who are you? Why are you here every day?"

Arthur instantly understood. His heart skipped a beat. Then he smiled with great tenderness and love and replied: "What I have to tell you is not easy to understand. It may seem impossible to accept. But if you'll listen to my story— if you're willing to trust me—then maybe in the end you'll believe me. And it's very important that you, in particular, should believe me. For without knowing it, you're the only person in the world who can share my secret."

Acknowledgments

Nathalie André, Paul Boujenah, Kamel Berkane,
Bernard Fixot, Philippe Guez, Rébecca Hayat, Raymond
and Danièle Levy, Lorraine Levy, Rémi Mangin, Coco
Miller, Manon Sbaïz, and Aline Souliers
and
Bernard Barrault, Greer Kessel Hendricks, and Susanna Lea.

About the Author

Marc Levy was born and bred in France. *Just Like Heaven* was his first novel: published in thirty-two languages, it became an international bestseller, selling more than 3 million copies worldwide.